The date

"I want to see Zach," said Chloe, who was bored. "Can't I even talk to him?"

"Chloe, I would advise you not to do anything. Go along with the process. This is prom. Lots of people get fixed up."

"But what if I hate him?" said Chloe, sticking her finger in her water glass again. "Or what if he's gorgeous and I fall hopelessly in love with him and he thinks I'm a freak? That's probably what'll happen. Oh my God. This is going to be a disaster."

"If you don't act like a freak, he won't think you are one," said Laura. "Take your finger out of your water."

~

OTHER SPEAK BOOKS

prom anonymous

BLAKE NELSON

speak
An Imprint of Penguin Group (USA) Inc.

nel

SPEAK

Published by the Penguin Group

Penguin Group (USA) Inc., 345 Hudson Street, New York, New York 10014, U.S.A.
Penguin Group (Canada), 90 Eglinton Avenue East, Suite 700,
Toronto, Ontario, Canada M4P 2Y3 (a division of Pearson Penguin Canada Inc.)
Penguin Books Ltd, 80 Strand, London WC2R 0RL, England
Penguin Ireland, 25 St Stephen's Green, Dublin 2, Ireland
(a division of Penguin Books Ltd)
Penguin Group (Australia), 250 Camberwell Road, Camberwell, Victoria 3124, Australia
(a division of Pearson Australia Group Pty Ltd)
Penguin Books India Pvt Ltd, 11 Community Centre, Panchsheel Park,
New Delhi - 110 017, India
Penguin Group (NZ), Cnr Airborne and Rosedale Roads, Albany,
Auckland 1310, New Zealand (a division of Pearson New Zealand Ltd)
Penguin Books (South Africa) (Pty) Ltd, 24 Sturdee Avenue,
Rosebank, Johannesburg 2196, South Africa

Registered Offices: Penguin Books Ltd, 80 Strand, London WC2R 0RL, England

First published in the United States of America by Viking,
a division of Penguin Young Readers Group, 2006
Published by Speak, an imprint of Penguin Group (USA) Inc., 2007

1 3 5 7 9 10 8 6 4 2

Copyright © Blake Nelson, 2006

THE LIBRARY OF CONGRESS HAS CATALOGED THE VIKING EDITION AS FOLLOWS:
Nelson, Blake, date–
Prom anonymous / by Blake Nelson.
p. cm.
Summary: Three childhood friends reunite to attend prom together and, in the
process of finding dates and dresses, gain some surprising insights into themselves.
ISBN 0-670-05945-5
[1. Proms—Fiction. 2. Interpersonal relations—Fiction. 3. Self-confidence—Fiction.
4. High schools—Fiction. 5. Schools—Fiction.] I. Title.
PZ7.N4328Pro 2006 [Fic]—dc22 2005007611

Speak ISBN 978-0-14-240745-5

Printed in the United States of America

For my mom

THANK YOU: Regina Hayes and Catherine Frank, Charlotte Sheedy, Carolyn Kim, Kirby Kim. Also big thanks to the lovely Beth Rosenberg, the always perfectly behaved girls of Kent Place School, and all the people who shared their embarrassing prom stories with me.

She paused at the top of the staircase. The sensations attributed to divers on spring-boards, leading ladies on opening nights, and lumpy, husky young men on the day of the Big Game, crowded through her. . . . She had never been so curious about her appearance, she had never been so satisfied with it. She had been sixteen years old for six months. . . . —F. Scott Fitzgerald

It's up to me now, turn on the bright lights. —Interpol

LAURA'S PROM CHART

```
~ KEY ~

F .......... Friend
PF ......... Primary Friend
NPR ....... Non-Prom Friend
D .......... Date
```

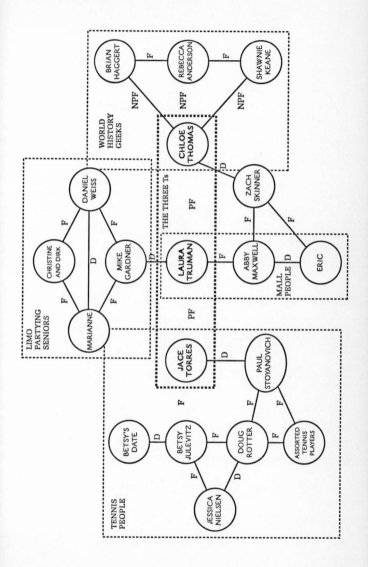

THE THREE TS:

In the photograph, the three eighth-graders stand together in a line. The "Three Ts" they are called: Chloe Thomas, Julia "Jace" Torres, Laura Truman. They wear gym shorts, sweatshirts, kneesocks. It's Field Day, and they each hold up a blue ribbon, though it is Jace who actually won the competitions. She is the athlete of the group. She is a "natural" at almost everything she attempts, though on this day there is a hint of strain in her face. Her mother passed away the year before, and it is clear she still struggles with it every day.

Chloe Thomas, on her right, smiles more openly. Her shoulders are bony, and a row of silver braces lines her teeth. Her yellowish-blonde hair, parted on the side, is held in place by a thick red barrette. As an eighth-grader she is known as an "odd duck," a kicker of boys; her scrappy feistiness has not yet joined itself to the artistic sensibilities that will eventually define her.

On Jace's left is Laura Truman. Blonde, blue-eyed, she is the beauty of the group. She is an intelligent, careful *girl, even at thirteen. The photo is her idea. She is always organizing things, remembering things; her clarity of mind is a perfect match for Chloe's volatility and Jace's athletic adventurousness.*

The Three Ts, after sitting together in alphabetical school rows for eight years, are as close as sisters in this last year before high school, before boys, before the pressures of emerging adulthood begin pulling them away from one another. . . .

☑ DATES
◯ PREP
◯ PROM

1

Chloe Thomas was being fixed up.

She lay on the bed, on her stomach, her head propped up, her chin resting on her hand. In front of her lay a pen over a blank notebook page. Earlier she'd had an idea for a poem. She wanted to write it but then this *thing* had happened. Her two oldest friends, Laura and Jace, had taken her to McDonald's after school. And they'd talked her into going to the prom.

Now they were trying to find her a date.

"She's a junior, she's . . . I don't know, five-seven?" Laura said into her cell phone.

Chloe stared at the blank notebook page.

"Of course she's cute." Laura paced the room while she talked. Jace sat in a chair, flipping through the Evergreen yearbook of the year before.

"A lot of people asked her," said Laura into her phone. "She didn't want to. She's a little . . . unconventional."

Chloe touched the red plastic barrette that held her hair to one side. She wondered if she'd made the right decision. Her hero, the poet Sylvia Plath, had made two crucial decisions in her life: to get married, and to kill herself. Were the two decisions linked? Scholars debated it. Chloe did not. Trying to be normal did not always work for certain people.

"If they want to see what she looks like," said Jace from her chair, "tell them to look at last year's yearbook. Page one forty-seven."

Laura ignored this. "Really?" she said into the phone. "What's he like? . . . No, that might be okay. . . . In a band? Yeah? . . . No, she's not goth. . . . She's not like that. . . . All in black? . . . No, no, she isn't going to wear *black leather* to the prom. . . ."

Chloe rolled onto her back. She looked at the ceiling. The paint on it was blotchy and uneven. *Spackled*, they called that. Chloe liked the word *spackled*.

"What about the other guy?" Laura said into her phone. "What's he like?"

Jace tried to show Laura the picture of Chloe in the yearbook. It was the page for their school's literary magazine, *Windsong*. "Maybe we could scan it," whispered Jace. "And then we could e-mail it to people."

Laura looked at it. "It's not the most flattering," she whispered.

"I think it's okay," said Jace.

Laura addressed Chloe directly. "Do you have any good digital photos of yourself?"

Chloe shook her head no.

"We could take some," suggested Jace.

Laura was getting another call. She clicked over. "Hello? Andy?" she said, adopting a calm, professional tone. "Hi. I'm Michelle's friend Laura? . . . Right, right. . . . I called because I have a friend and she doesn't have a date for our prom and Michelle said you were going and maybe you knew someone?"

Chloe blinked up at the ceiling. *She was going to the prom.* She tried to picture it: the excited crowds, the dresses, the boys in tuxedos. People would rent limos and hotel rooms and have extravagant parties, all in hopes of creating a perfect moment, a perfect memory they could bury away in their brains. The pursuit of memories was what youth was to most people, everything done for that video camera in your soul: *Look at me! Look at how I used to be! Look at the people I used to love!*

"Her bra size is none of your business," said Laura, into the phone. "Gawwd!"

Jace was looking at a different picture in the yearbook now.

"Yeah?" said Laura, to a new caller. "A swimmer? . . . No, that would be okay. What's he like? . . . Uh-huh. . . . The thing is, she's very artistic. She can't be with a total jock. . . . No, no, nerdy is okay, as long as it's *artsy* nerdy, not computer nerdy."

Chloe tried not to listen. She rolled back onto her stomach, returning to her notebook, to her poem. But the idea was gone. She doodled in the margin instead. She wondered at what she'd gotten herself into.

2

Even without her trademark plastic barrette, Chloe Thomas was a strange girl to look at. She had a round pumpkin face; thick, uncontrollable blonde hair; intense green eyes that many at Evergreen High School found unnerving. She was thin, pale, and obviously "artistic," though she did not dress in any particular style to indicate this. She considered punk too obvious, goth too dramatic, emo too doctrinaire. She did not wear dark makeup or neckties or ripped-up T-shirts, or any of the usual things teenage girls used to express their outrage at the world. No, Chloe made her own Chloe-esque statement by scowling a lot, hiding behind her hair, and dressing herself in the most random outfits imaginable. That night, for example, as she entered Barnes & Noble, she wore a pair of blue "EZ-Stretch" polyester pants (Salvation Army), red pajama tops (JCPenney), a light brown sweater vest (a trunk in her grandfather's attic), a pair of black PRO-Keds (the outlet mall) and pink skull socks (Hot Topic).

Inside the Barnes & Noble, Chloe followed her familiar route to the world history section. She and a small gang of other Evergreen misfits had made it their hangout.

Already present that night were Shawnie Keane and Rebecca Anderson. They both mumbled greetings as Chloe took her usual place on the carpeted floor. Rebecca, in her oversized military coat, was curled up with a copy of *Fantasy Quest Magazine*. Shawnie, who had dyed blue hair and rings through her tongue and lower lip, busily worked on an original female action hero she hoped might grace the cover of that semester's *Windsong*.

Minutes later, Brian Haggert appeared with a grande mocha latte from the Starbucks next door. "Oh my God, there you are!" he said when he saw Chloe. "I just got your message. I can't believe you're doing that!"

This attracted the attention of Shawnie and Rebecca.

"Tell me about it," said Brian, as he dumped his backpack on the floor. "How did they talk you into it?"

Chloe shrugged.

"Talk you into what?" said Shawnie.

"She's going to the prom!" said Brian.

"You're doing *what*?" said Shawnie. "But you said you hated proms. You said you would never go."

"I know," said Chloe, simply. "I changed my mind."

"What did they say?" asked Brian. "How did they talk you into it?"

Chloe scribbled in her notebook. "They said I would regret it someday," she said. "They said I would look back and there would be a big hole in my life where prom was supposed to be."

"And you *believed* that?" said Shawnie.

"No," said Chloe. "But they really wanted me to go. They used to be my best friends."

"Yeah, like in *eighth grade*," said Brian. "That's a long time ago."

Chloe shrugged again. "Maybe it'll be fun. Maybe I want to see what it's like."

"Proms are *not* fun," said Shawnie. "Nothing happens at proms except boys get drunk and girls get date-raped."

Chloe ignored this. "If everyone thinks it's such an important event, there must be *something* about it. . . ."

"Listen to you!" said Brian. "You're really going. I can't believe it. You're so brave!"

"That's not bravery, that's selling out!" declared Shawnie. "I would never go to the prom. People who are into prom are the worst people of all."

"I don't know if I would go," said Rebecca, quietly, curling her fists in the sleeves of her military coat. "No guy would ask me, so it doesn't matter."

"Guys don't ask you because you're not a brainless Barbie doll," said Shawnie. "Guys want girls who will have sex with them, girls who are so grateful someone asked them, they'll do anything in return."

Rebecca listened to this but did not believe it. She was a small, timid girl, though she did wear a button on her coat that said, "Girls Kick Ass." Everyone loved that button. Chloe sometimes borrowed it.

"I can't believe you," continued Shawnie. "I would *never* go to prom. Not for *any* reason."

"Yeah, but you're just afraid," said Brian.

"I'm not afraid of anything," sneered Shawnie, which was true enough. Just last week Shawnie had beaten up a girl outside Starbucks for making fun of her hair.

"I understand what you're doing," said Rebecca, thoughtfully. "You're going as an experiment. You're going as an artist."

"I went to the all-city gay prom last year," said Brian. "It was pretty great, I have to admit."

"See? Now *that* I would go to," said Shawnie, returning to her female superhero.

Chloe continued with her own drawing. "The only thing is, who will I go with?"

"Go with a girl. That would mess with their heads," said Shawnie.

"Are you going to ask someone?" asked Rebecca.

"Laura said she would fix me up," said Chloe.

"Really? You would go with someone you didn't know?" said Rebecca.

"They said it doesn't matter who you go with," said Chloe. "It's more about the ritual."

Rebecca gazed at Chloe for a long time. "I can't believe you're really going to the prom."

"You're brave," repeated Brian.

"You're insane," said Shawnie.

3

Laura Truman strolled easily beside Mike Gardner, her boyfriend of fourteen months. It was a bright sunny day, the first nice day of a rainy Oregon spring. As they walked, Laura told Mike the exciting news: She had convinced her old friend Chloe to come to the prom.

Mike, a tall, handsome senior, was less than thrilled. "When did this happen?" he asked, as they crossed Evergreen's parking lot.

"Last night," said Laura. "It was so weird. Jace and I were ready to try all these different arguments, you know, to convince her. But we'd barely started and she said yes."

"And now I suppose we have to go with her," said Mike.

Laura looked at him with surprise. "Of course we have to go with her; she's one of my oldest friends. She was one of the Three Ts."

"Yeah, but it's not like you guys hang out now."

Laura frowned. "She is still a very important person to me. And she always will be."

"Until you graduate."

"*Forever.* I've been friends with her since *grade school.*"

Mike shook his head. "What about Daniel and Marianne and those guys? They don't want to hang out with Chloe Thomas. And they're the people *I* want to go with."

"We can see them when we get there."

"But I don't want to just *see* them. I want to hang with them. They're the ones who'll be partying, and having the most fun."

"You can still party with them," reasoned Laura. "We'll meet them when we get there."

Mike walked. He pulled out his car keys. "They're doing a senior chill room this year."

"Really?" said Laura. She was surprised by this. Two years before, they'd had a "chill room" at prom, but people had tried to smuggle booze in and they'd shut it down.

"Daniel helped arrange it," said Mike. "It'll be like our own personal VIP area. Seniors only. We can totally party. We can do whatever we want."

"You're not going to try to sneak anything in are you?" Laura asked.

"We won't have to if we plan it right. The point is, after all these years, we'll finally get to do it up right."

"No, it sounds fun," agreed Laura.

"But not if we have Chloe Thomas following us around," said Mike. They had arrived at his Jeep Cherokee. He unlocked it with his remote.

"Chloe's not that bad."

"Are you kidding? Have you seen the people she hangs out with? Shawnie Keane? And that Brian guy?

That dude wears *eyeliner.* I'm not going *anywhere* with him, in case you have any ideas about that."

"He's not even going."

They both got in the Cherokee. Mike started the engine. "I'm telling you," said Mike, backing out of the parking space, "this would be a lot more fun with Daniel and Marianne and those guys. We'll have a limo. And champagne. We can hit the after-parties."

"We can still do that."

"With Chloe Thomas? How do you figure?"

Laura sighed. "To be honest, I didn't think you'd care that much," she said. "As long as you and I were together."

Mike put the car in drive and pulled away. "Yeah. Whatever. I just want to have fun this year."

Laura glared at him. "What did you say?"

"I said I want to have fun this year."

"Did you just *whatever* me? When I said we would be together? Like you didn't even care?"

"I'm just *saying,*" argued Mike. "We've done this before. We went last year. And we had a great time, didn't we?"

Laura said nothing.

"Didn't we?" said Mike. "And we did all the romantic stuff. We had dinner at the whatchamacallit, on top of the hotel. And we went to the beach house afterward, with the candlelight and all that."

Laura stared forward.

"All I'm saying," continued Mike, "is it might be fun

to do more social stuff this time. Marianne and Christine will be there; it's not like there won't be girls."

"Marianne will get plastered."

"So what? She likes to party. What's wrong with that? She's a senior. *I'm* a senior. That's what seniors do."

"If that's how you feel," said Laura. "If you think the romantic part of our relationship is over."

"Come on," said Mike. "We've been going out for *two years.*"

"Fourteen months," Laura corrected him.

"Fourteen months. You know what I mean."

"I don't care," said Laura. "*I'm* still a junior and Chloe and Jace have never been to prom, and I want to experience it with them. They're going to need me."

"People don't need you as much as you think," said Mike.

Laura glared at him for a moment. But she didn't want to fight. She looked out her window.

"Who's Jace going with?" asked Mike, in a quieter tone.

"That transfer guy, Paul," said Laura. "That's who she wants to go with. She's having trouble asking him though. He thinks they're just friends."

"Paul? Paul who?"

"He's on the tennis team."

"Oh yeah, that blond kid. From California."

"Supposedly he's great at tennis."

"Yeah," grumbled Mike. "California people. They're always good at everything."

Mike drove the two of them to his house. Unfortunately, both of Mike's parents' cars were in the driveway, which meant both were home, which meant he and Laura couldn't hang out in the basement. So Mike kept driving. He drove down the hill and into the woods behind Raleigh Park. Laura knew where they were going.

Mike parked in the usual spot. He got out and got in the backseat. When Laura didn't immediately follow, he frowned at her. "Now what's the matter?" he asked.

"Nothing. I'm coming."

She opened her door and got into the backseat with him. She took off her coat and scooted across the seat, preparing herself for what was coming. First, they kissed. Then Mike reached under her shirt and squeezed her breasts. He undid his belt and pulled down his pants like he always did and she touched it, like she always did.

He got out the condom, and she slipped off her pants and positioned herself the way he liked. He was fast when they did it in the car, in the woods. She was glad for that today. She wanted to get home. She looked out the window while Mike had sex with her. Then she felt guilty she wasn't paying more attention. She tried to moan and arch her back, the way people said you should. *Act sexy for your boyfriend.* Mike didn't really notice, anyway. It was like he was in his own little world lately. Maybe that was what happened when you did it a lot. She had recently calculated that they had had sex over a hundred times (two times a week, fifty weeks). It was amazing when you thought about it.

Mike began to grunt the way he did. He was getting close. Laura always found this part touching. She stroked his hair, breathed softly into his ear.

When he was finished, he conked out for a few minutes, as usual. She lay beneath him, staring at the Jeep's ceiling, at the interior light. It had two separate directional lights, like an airplane, so one person could read while the other person drove. That's what they had done last month when they went to Mike's beach house. Laura did homework while Mike drove and said nothing and thought about whatever boys think about when they drive long distances.

4

At home, Laura threw her books down in the family room and yelled upstairs to her mother. The local news was on the TV in the kitchen, and she stopped for a moment to watch the five-day weather forecast. More rain was on the way, showers, overcast skies. Prom was still nearly three weeks away; hopefully it would be warmer by then. Not that it mattered. Last year it had rained and Laura remembered it only enhanced the glamour of the event:

the tearlike raindrops on Mike's windshield, the excited dash across the wet street to the ballroom. She was a sophomore then, an unknown at her school, going with Mike, a popular junior. It truly had been a night she would never forget—which was exactly why she had to help her friends this year.

She got a glass of milk from the fridge and went upstairs to her mother's room. Mrs. Truman was doing something at her worktable. Laura's grandmother, Nana, sat behind her on the bed, watching Oprah on TV.

Laura flopped on the bed beside her nana. "You'll never believe what I did yesterday," she said.

"What?" said her mother.

"I talked Chloe Thomas into going to the prom."

"Oh, my," said Nana.

"Didn't she want to go?" said Mrs. Truman.

"No way," said Laura, drinking milk. "You know how she is now. She won't do anything normal."

"Little Chloe Thomas?" said Nana.

"She's not so little anymore," Laura's mother said. "She's all grown-up and she's weird as a bat."

"She's just having an artistic phase," corrected Laura.

"How did you convince her?" asked her mother.

"She sort of convinced herself," said Laura. "We barely said a word."

"Maybe she really wanted to go," said Mrs. Truman. "She just needed a little prompting."

"Maybe," said Laura. She picked up the crossword

puzzle book her grandmother had been working on.

"How's Mike?" said her mom. "Is he getting excited?"

"Not really."

"Why not?"

"He says we already had our romantic prom last year, and this year he wants to party more."

"What kind of partying does he mean?" asked Laura's mother with concern.

"Nothing bad," said Laura, flipping through the crossword book. "Typical prom stuff. Limos. Restaurants. He wants us to go with Daniel Weiss and those guys."

"And you want to go with Chloe and Jace?"

"That was the plan."

"Don't lose my puzzle," said Nana.

"Oh. Sorry," said Laura, flipping back, trying to find Nana's puzzle.

"You and Mike have been together a long time," said Laura's mother. "I can see why he'd want to be with his other friends, too."

"I know," said Laura. "I guess we can do both."

"What about your dress?" asked her grandmother.

"I wanted to ask you about that, actually," said Laura.

"You heard your father," said Mrs. Truman. "You can get a new dress, but you're not to spend more than two hundred dollars."

"But, *Mom*," said Laura. "That should be *my* choice. Dad already said."

"He said you can *choose* it this year. But he doesn't

want you spending a ton of money on it."

"But it's *my* prom. And it's *my* money," said Laura. She looked at her grandmother. "What do you think, Nana?"

"I don't think you'll remember the money. You will always remember your prom."

"See, Mom? *See?* Your own mother?"

"In Nana's day people didn't waste thousands of dollars on proms," advised Laura's mother. "Two hundred dollars is plenty."

"But you can't get *anything* for two hundred dollars," said Laura, flipping through the crossword puzzle book again.

"Who's Chloe going with?" said her mother.

"We're trying to find someone," said Laura.

"Is there someone she wants to go with?"

"She doesn't care. She wants us to pick."

"That's no way to go to a prom," scoffed Nana.

"That's how she is," said Laura. "Her parents will be glad, though. They think she's gay."

"Lau-ra!" scolded Mrs. Truman.

"What?" said Laura. "It's true. They had gay people in your day, didn't they, Nana?"

"Not in high school," said her grandmother.

"I don't know what's going to happen," said Laura. "I just want everyone to have a great time. I want Jace and Chloe to see how fun it is."

"Just remember, honey," said her mother, "everyone

has to experience things their own way. Don't let this become like your knitting club. You know how that turned out."

"I know, I know," said Laura. "I'm too *controlling*."

5

Julia "Jace" Torres gripped her tennis racquet and stared across the net at her opponents. Ahead 6–1, 5–3, she needed one more game to win her doubles match. Unfortunately she had developed a bad case of the jitters. Jace had double-faulted twice, and her partner, Betsy Julevitz, had hit her last two volleys into the net.

"C'mon, Jace, relax out there!" barked Mr. Hawkins, the Evergreen tennis coach. "Easy motion now! Stay fluid!"

It was doubly embarrassing because this was Glencoe, who had the worst tennis team in the Metro League. Jace and Betsy should have been winning easily. Jace tossed the ball and swung. The ball hit the net. *Crap*, she thought.

"C'mon, Torres," called one of the boy players. Her doubles match was one of the last of the day, and the other Evergreen players were watching. Worst of all: Paul Stoyanovich, the boys' number-one singles player, was among them. He stood at her end of the court, slouched against the fence, his fingers entwined in the chain-link.

He was making Jace very nervous. Why couldn't he be watching her play basketball? She was the star point guard on the varsity team. She was terrible at tennis.

Her wimpy second serve went in. If the opposing players had been any good they would have killed it. Fortunately, they weren't. The return was high and went right to Betsy. She smashed it for a winner. *Thank God,* thought Jace.

The game was tied.

Jace bounced the ball and again thought how ridiculous she must look to Paul Stoyanovich. This time, though, the thought motivated her. Jace tossed the ball, arched her back, and hit a solid first serve. The opposing girl missed it, and the point was won.

"Way to go, Torres!" said Coach Hawkins.

"Get 'em, Jace!" said another boy player. Several of the boys were watching now. Jace moved to the opposite side and prepared for the final point.

"Serve to the backhand," said a different voice behind her as she bounced the ball. It was Paul's voice.

"Thanks, *Paul*," said Jace, not looking at him. A couple of the guys laughed.

"No distractions," called Mr. Hawkins from the side of the court. "C'mon guys, let 'em finish."

Jace served to the backhand. The Glencoe girl hit it back but it was a weak, shallow shot. Betsy sprang for it, slammed it, and won the match.

"Yes!" cried Jace from the service line.

"Yes!" said Betsy, making a fist.

Jace, always a good sport, immediately squelched her excitement and ran to the net to shake hands.

"Thank God you guys finally won," whispered one of the Glencoe girls. "I gotta get home. I'm picking up my prom dress tonight."

"You guys have prom this week?" whispered Betsy.

"Friday. And I still don't have my dress. She does, though," indicating her partner.

"Oh my God, you guys," said the partner, "I have the best dress ever!"

"Our prom isn't till June," said Betsy.

"Are you both going?"

"I am," said Betsy. "She's trying for that guy over there. Paul. Behind the fence."

"Shhhh!" said Jace.

"Oh yeah," whispered the first Glencoe girl. "I saw him before; he's cute."

"I know. She's afraid to ask him, though," said Betsy.

"I am not!" hissed Jace. "I'm just waiting for the right time."

The four of them walked off the court and stood at the bench, toweling off.

"You just have to go for it," advised the Glencoe girl. "I asked this guy who I never thought would go with me. And he said yes."

"Really?" said Jace, sneaking a look at the far end of the court. Paul was walking to the end court to watch the last of the boys' doubles.

"Is there anything we can do to help?" asked the Glencoe girl.

"No," said Jace. "I just gotta do it. Thanks, though."

"Sorry we beat you," said Betsy.

"That's okay," said the girl. "We don't care. We only play because our parents make us."

6

Jace and Betsy hurried into the Glencoe locker room to change. Jace stood at the mirror washing her face. Though she was naturally cute—creamy bronze skin, almond brown eyes—Jace was utterly clueless in the art of primping. Even when her mother was alive she had been a tomboy and a jock. Now, with Paul in the picture, she had to change that. She borrowed some lip gloss from Betsy.

Betsy stepped outside to check on Paul's location. "He's watching the boys now," she reported. "They're in the last set. You'd better hurry."

"Oh God," said Jace, checking her lips in the mirror. "Oh God, oh God, oh God."

"Don't worry. This is perfect. He's standing by himself."

Jace Torres straightened herself and went outside.

Betsy followed close behind. "Tell him about Chloe," she said. "That's the perfect excuse to bring it up. Talk about Chloe and keep saying 'prom.' Say the word 'prom' over and over."

"Prom . . . prom . . . prom . . . prom," said Jace.

"Perfect," said Betsy.

Jace marched across the grass. Paul stood by himself, watching the last of the boys' doubles. She almost lost her nerve as she approached him. She glanced behind her, but Betsy had discreetly vanished. Jace was on her own.

She forced herself forward. She looked at the grass beneath her feet. *I'm just going to talk to him,* she said to herself. *Just like I always do.*

She came up behind him. "Hey, Paul," she said, her voice suddenly tight in her throat.

"Hey," he answered. "Nice game."

"No it wasn't," she said. "We were terrible. They were just worse than us."

"They weren't as bad as my guy," said Paul, smiling.

"Glencoe isn't very good at tennis," said Jace. "They're more farm kids. They're good at football." That was how she had become friends with Paul, explaining stuff to him, about their school, about their league. He had only transferred in last semester, so he needed the help.

"So," said Jace, taking a short breath. "You know my friend Chloe? Who I was telling you about?"

"The girl you wanted to go to the prom?"

"Well guess what?" said Jace. "We did it!"

"She said she would go?"

"She did!"

"Nice," said Paul. "How'd you do that?"

"We sat her down and started telling her all the reasons she should go. And before we could even finish, she said yes."

"Nice," said Paul.

Jace watched him say this. She loved his smile. He got this crinkle on one side of his face. She also loved how he said "nice" all the time. It was very California, and totally adorable.

Jace swallowed once and continued. "So now all we have to do is get her a date."

"How are you going to do that?" asked Paul.

"Laura's doing it. She thinks getting a guy from another school is the best way. Because a lot of guys think, like . . . well, that Chloe's a little weird."

"Huh," said Paul.

"So Laura's calling around. Hopefully we can find someone kind of quirky or whatever. Someone she can have a good time with."

"Sounds good," said Paul.

"Yeah. Except there's still one problem."

"What's that?"

"Well, I still . . . I mean . . . I don't actually . . . because Laura has Mike who she's gone out with forever . . . so, I still would need . . . or still need to find . . . you know . . . a person . . ."

"You don't have a date?" said Paul, genuinely surprised.

"Right," said Jace with relief. "I don't have a date."

Paul seemed to think about this. But he didn't say anything. He turned and watched the tennis.

"I mean, I could find someone," said Jace, pressing on. "A guy friend or whatever. The thing is, I kinda think you should only go with a guy friend if you have to. You know, like if there's someone you might *like* . . ." Jace pulled on her index finger as she said this. "It seems like a waste to pick some guy you've known forever. Don't you think?"

"I guess," said Paul, not looking at her.

"What about you?" Jace suddenly blurted. She said it so fast she surprised herself.

"Am I going?" he said.

Then, at the worst possible moment, there was a commotion on the court in front of them. "That was out!" shouted an Evergreen player.

"No it wasn't," said the Glencoe player.

"It was out by six inches."

"It was in. I saw it."

"Hey, Paul!" said the Evergreen boy. "Did you see that ball?"

Paul stared through the fence at them.

"You can't ask him; he's on your team," protested the Glencoe player.

"So what? He's closest."

"Sorry guys, I didn't see it," said Paul.

"It was out."

"It was in."

"How about you, Torres?" asked the other Evergreen player.

Jace shook her head. "Sorry. I didn't see it, either."

"Play it over," said the Glencoe guy.

"It was *out*."

"Play it over for chrissakes!"

Paul turned back to Jace. "A girl in my history class asked me. I said no."

"Someone already asked you?" said Jace in horror.

Paul didn't notice. "I figured, since I'm a transfer, and I don't really have any history here . . ."

"But you've been here almost a year," protested Jace. "That's some history. And you can still go. It's just about having fun." She pulled on her index finger again.

"I dunno," said Paul. "I don't like crowded events."

Jace tried desperately to think of another way to make her point. It was no use. Paul was watching the tennis now. The moment had passed. She'd blown it. Again.

7

"Chloe? Is that you?" said her mother.

"Yes," said Chloe, lugging her backpack into the kitchen and dropping it against the wall.

"Chloe, honey? I'm going to yoga late tonight. I made some soup for you and your brother to heat up."

"Okay," said Chloe. Her little brother, Dylan, was playing a video game in the TV room. Her dad, a college professor, was in his study, working on his book about medieval arches.

"Honey, did you hear me?" said Mrs. Thomas, coming into the kitchen. She wore sandals and a baggy black sweater. Her silver-streaked hair was pulled back in a ponytail.

"Okay," said Chloe.

"How is everybody? How's Shawnie?"

Chloe shrugged. "You know how she beat up that girl at Starbucks?"

"Yes?"

"That girl's parents are suing Shawnie's parents."

"Are they really?" said her mother. She was trying to get her mineral water into her Guatemalan travel bag with her yoga mat, her art supplies, and her copy of *The Da Vinci Code*.

"That's what the girl claimed," said Chloe.

"Well, that's what happens when you resort to violence. I think Shawnie has some real issues with aggression. I wonder if her parents are taking that seriously enough."

"What can they do?" said Chloe. "She already goes to therapy three times a week."

Chloe's little brother wandered into the kitchen. He sat on a stool and dropped his head dramatically down on the kitchen counter.

"Dylan? Are you okay?" said his mother.

"*Yes.*"

"What's wrong, honey?"

"I lost again."

"What did you lose?"

"I lost at Darkanian. I can never get over ten thousand. Claude gets twenty thousand every time he plays. And he always kills the Sorceress. I haven't killed her once."

"Sweetie, why do you have to kill people to have fun?"

"The Sorceress isn't a person. She's an Angel of Darkness," whined Dylan. "And if you don't kill her, she kills you."

Mrs. Thomas went back to her packing. "You know how I feel about violent computer games."

"Mom?" said Chloe, her voice straining slightly.

"Yes, Chloe?"

"Can I talk to you?"

"I'm kind of running out the door."

"I know. When you get back?"

"Sure, honey," said her mother. "What is it? Something important?"

"Kind of."

"Can it wait until I get back?"

"Yeah," said Chloe. "I guess."

Her mother could hear the emotion in her daughter's voice. "Or is it something you need to tell me now?"

"I don't know," said Chloe. There was a tension in Chloe's face Mrs. Thomas had never seen before.

"Well," said Mrs. Thomas, checking her watch. "We have a few minutes. I have to get a bigger bag, anyway. Can you come upstairs?"

Chloe followed her mother upstairs to her room. Mrs. Thomas went to her closet and dug out a larger bag. Chloe sat on the bed and watched her mother. "So what is it, honey?" said her mom.

When Chloe didn't answer, Mrs. Thomas turned toward her daughter. Chloe sat silently on the bed. Her mother went to her, sat with her. "Sweetie? What is it?"

"It's nothing really. . . ."

"Honey, listen. You know how much your father and I love you. You can tell us whatever it is. Any feelings you're having. Of any kind. You don't have to be ashamed."

Chloe frowned. Her parents had recently given her the If-You're-Gay-We-Still-Love-You lecture. "No, Mom, I told you, I'm not gay."

"Well what is it then, honey? You can tell me. Whatever it is."

"It's sort of weird," said Chloe.

"That's okay. What is it?"

"I'm . . . I'm going to the prom," said Chloe quietly.

Her mother's face went blank. "You're what?"

"I'm going to the prom."

"You are?"

Chloe nodded. "Laura and Jace wanted me to go with them. So I said yes."

Mrs. Thomas studied her daughter. She and her husband had just that week talked to yet another counselor about their increasingly withdrawn daughter. First there had been the Sylvia Plath obsession, then she quit all her after-school activities, and lately her only friends were the two most antisocial girls in her class and the school's only openly gay student.

And now she was going to the prom?

"Wait," said Mrs. Thomas. "Let me get this straight. You? Chloe? Are going to the prom?"

Chloe nodded.

Her mother tried not to look so stunned. "Well that's great, honey! That'll be fun. Won't it?"

"I don't know. I never went to one before."

"Well, that's probably a good reason to try it," said Mrs. Thomas, as she studied her inexplicable daughter.

"But I'm scared. I won't know what to do," said Chloe.

"Don't worry, honey," said her mother. She stood up and went to the bedroom door. "David!" she called downstairs to her husband. "Would you come up here a minute?"

"What is it?" called her husband from his study.

"There's something Chloe wants to tell you!"

Mr. Thomas appeared in the bedroom within seconds. "Yes?" he said. He worried about Chloe even more than his wife. It was he who had become convinced that Chloe was gay.

"Chloe's going to the prom!" said Mrs. Thomas, unable to contain her excitement.

Mr. Thomas's face went from deep concern to disbelieving happiness.

"The prom? Like . . . at her—?"

"The *prom*," said Mrs. Thomas triumphantly. "Her high school prom. At her own school!"

Chloe tried to smile at her father, but she had her usual trouble with eye contact. Her father didn't notice. He was doing his best to contain himself. He did not want to hope for too much, but the joy spreading through him was obvious. Maybe his daughter was coming back. Maybe she would be his little girl again. Maybe, well, he didn't know. He only knew that this was the best news he'd had all year.

His daughter was going to the prom!

8

"So who are you going with?" Chloe's father asked. This was the next logical question, but it came out of his mouth quickly; it sounded almost accusatory. His wife frowned at him.

Chloe answered the question. "Laura and Jace," she said. She stared at her shoes as she spoke.

"Oh," said Mr. Thomas.

"I mean, I'll go with a boy," Chloe assured him. "You have to. They don't let you go without a date."

"Do you know who your date will be?" asked her mother, more cautiously.

"Laura is helping me. She's going to find someone."

Her mother nodded her encouragement. "Well, good for Laura. She's always been a good friend to you."

"I guess I'll need some money and stuff," said Chloe. "If you want I could do some extra work around the house. . . ."

"Don't worry about money," said Mr. Thomas, eagerly. "Whatever it costs, we can handle it."

"We'll give it to you as an early birthday present," said her mom.

"Never mind presents, we're just giving it to you," said Mr. Thomas, who seemed to think Chloe's announcement was *his* birthday present. He took a seat beside her on the bed. "Honey, this is great. This is fantastic. Whatever you need, we'll get for you."

Chloe, as was her nature, resisted this outpouring of generosity. "You just want to help me because you think I'm a freak."

Mrs. Thomas put her arms around her daughter. "Chloe! Don't ever say that. We have *never* thought you were a freak. You're bright and you're sensitive and you're creative and we love you to death. We just worry sometimes that you're not having as much fun as a girl your age should have. You seem so determined not to enjoy yourself, it worries us sometimes."

"What do you need at a prom, anyway?" said Mr. Thomas, trying to remember his own prom experiences.

Chloe untangled herself from her mother. "I don't really

know. Laura and Jace have been telling me stuff. You have to get a dress. And you get your nails done or whatever. A pedicure."

"A *manicure*," corrected her mother. "Pedicure is for your feet."

"Really?" said Chloe, raising her head. "What do they do to your feet?"

"Never mind."

"And a limo?" said her father. "I guess the boys take care of that."

"You're not going with Brian Haggert are you?" asked her mother.

"No, he goes to the gay prom."

"So you're actually going with a normal boy?" said her father, who still couldn't believe his good fortune.

"Or whoever Laura picks," said Chloe.

"What about you?" asked her mother. "Is there a boy you like?"

"Not really. That's why I want them to choose."

"Huh," said her dad.

"I think it's a very grown-up decision on your part," said her mother. "I'm proud of you for doing this. For taking a risk. For challenging yourself."

Chloe found this statement vaguely insulting. But she said nothing. She did what she always did during awkward interactions with people. She lowered her face so that her yellow hair fell forward and hid her from the world.

• • •

Later, from her room, Chloe called Brian Haggert.

"What did your parents say?" he asked.

"They about died," said Chloe. "They think it's the greatest thing ever. They think I'm *participating* now."

"In what?"

"Who knows. High school. Life. At least my dad said he'd give me money for a dress and stuff."

"What kind of dress will you get?"

"I don't know," said Chloe. "Whatever they have."

"Do you even know how to buy a real dress?"

"What's there to know?" said Chloe. "Don't you just buy it?"

"No, Chloe. You don't just buy it. Do you want me to help you?"

"I guess. If you want."

"Chloe?" said Brian. "No offense, but you're going to need *a lot* of help. This is a prom we're talking about. It's kind of involved."

"All right, if you don't mind."

"Not at all."

"It's so funny," Chloe said. "The minute I decided to do this, everyone wants to help me. Laura and Jace, my parents. And now you."

"What do you expect? People love you."

"I don't want people to love me."

"Well there's nothing you can do. They love you anyway."

Chloe studied her fingernails. "God, I'm going to have to buy all this crap. And get my nails done. This is already making my stomach hurt."

There was a loud knock at Chloe's door.

She covered the phone. "Yes?"

The door opened. Her brother, Dylan, stuck his head in.

"Can I help you?" said Chloe.

"Is it true?" he said. "You're going to the prom?"

"None of your business. Now go away, please."

"Are you crazy?" said Dylan. "Haven't you seen *Carrie*?"

"No, and I'm on the phone," said Chloe.

"You're gonna get *so killed*."

"No, I'm not."

"It's probably a trick. They'll probably get you onstage and drop pig's blood on you!"

"Thank you for being supportive," said Chloe, who lost all self-consciousness in fights with her brother. It was one of her favorite activities. "Now get out of my room, dickweed!"

"Chloe's going to the prom," sang Dylan.

"Get out! Now! Or I'm telling!"

"I'll tell Mom you said 'dickweed'!"

"I'll tell Mom you masturbate in your gym socks!"

"No you won't!"

"Mom!"

Dylan slammed the door. Chloe could hear him galloping down the hall.

"It's definitely shaking things up around the Thomas household," she told Brian.

"That makes it worth it right there."

9

Unlike Chloe, who didn't care about money, or Jace, whose dad gave her as much as she wanted, Laura would need extra money for the prom. She needed extra money for everything, which was why she had worked steadily at Staples all through high school and was now assistant manager at the store in Woodridge Mall.

That's where she was on Thursday night when one of the copy machines ran out of ink. As assistant manager, it was her job to replace it, which she did, though the big ink cartridges were ridiculously out of date. She got down on her hands and knees and began unhooking the old cartridge. That's when she saw Marianne and Christine strolling through the mall. On their arms hung shopping bags from Nordstrom's, Girl Talk, and most noticeably Victoria's Secret. The sight of the Victoria's Secret bag gave Laura a shiver. Both Marianne and Christine went out with friends of Mike Gardner, and by doing so, had become popular and important girls in the senior class. Before this year no normal people took them seriously: Marianne smoked, Christine shoplifted, and they both dressed too slutty. They were not like Laura, who had gained her reputation by being a good friend to people, being straightforward and nice and fun to hang out with. Marianne and Christine had taken a shortcut to social success. They had done it with sexiness, and with that strange confidence "bad" girls always seemed to have.

Laura considered it cheating somehow, and though she was always nice to Marianne and Christine, she didn't trust them. She didn't like what they stood for. She waited until they were gone before she stood up and lugged the old ink cartridge into the back.

Later, on her break, Laura walked through the mall to the shop she visited every day now: Springtime in Paris. That's where her prom dress was. Laura had put down the deposit, and she had the rest of the money. The problem was that she hadn't told her mother yet. The reason: The dress was $349. Of course, it was Laura's money; if this was what she wanted to spend it on, that was her right. Still, there would be a fight if Laura couldn't find some way to finesse things.

"Hello," said the saleswoman. She had helped Laura pick the dress out two weeks ago.

"Hi," said Laura. She gazed absently at the display version of her dress.

"Still look good to you?" said the woman.

"It's beautiful," said Laura, embarrassed. "I know. I should stop stalling. I have the money. I'm waiting to tell my mom."

"When's your prom?" asked the woman.

"Two weeks from tomorrow."

"Better not wait too long," said the woman.

"I know," said Laura. She touched the luxurious fabric. "Do you really think it's worth it?" she asked the woman. "I mean for one night?"

"Depends on you."

"Did you go to your prom?" asked Laura.

"Sure," said the woman, pleasantly. "It was great. I remember the dress. I remember everything."

"Who was your date?"

"He was a friend of a friend. I didn't know him too well. He was very cute, though. I see the pictures now and I think, why didn't I date that guy? It was still a wonderful night. The dancing, the dinner, all my friends."

"I guess that's the best part," said Laura.

"Well, if you have a nice guy, that's great, too."

"I do have a nice guy, actually. This'll be our second prom."

"Your second?" said the woman. "That's impressive. This really will be a special night."

Laura nodded and smiled as she thought about it.

"Well, whenever you're ready," said the woman. "We have yours in the back."

"Tomorrow," said Laura softly. "Tomorrow I think I'll be ready."

10

I may never be happy, but tonight I am content, Chloe said to herself as she walked across the Denny's parking lot. It was the first sentence in Sylvia Plath's *Collected Journals* and Chloe often repeated it to herself at odd times. Tonight it seemed more appropriate than usual. Chloe wasn't exactly *happy* about going to the prom. But in some strange way, it had filled up her life. It had made her feel real and whole and in the middle of things.

Chloe was meeting Jace and Laura. She opened the heavy door of Denny's and walked through the bright, air-conditioned restaurant. She liked Denny's. It was full of characters: truckers, local weirdos, the occasional brainiac high school student. Her friends were already there, waiting at a booth in the back.

Chloe joined them, and for a moment, the Three Ts grinned around the table at one another. How weird that they were hanging out again. And how fun.

"Okay," said Laura, getting down to business. "Here's what we have." Laura slid a piece of paper across the table to Jace and Chloe. The two girls studied the paper, which read:

TOP FIVE PROM DATE CHOICES:

GAVIN BROWN. *Goes to Glencoe. Senior, tall, not the best looking but super nice, recommended by Genevieve, who is going with his best friend (as friends). This is a very "friends" choice, as Genevieve does not think Gavin is looking for a relationship "in any way." He is in AP English and is considered smart (by Glencoe standards).*

MIKE KELLY. *Goes to Sunset. Junior. Friend of Abby Maxwell from the mall. Kind of a stoner, though not terrible, according to Abby. Easygoing. Would probably be into it, in a "whatever" kind of way. Wears one of those shell necklaces. Possibly too annoying in terms of hippieness, but would probably do whatever we told him.*

PETE NYUGEN. *Megan's old boyfriend. May be going anyway with Meg, so we have to check with her (she wants to go with someone else; Pete is her backup). Pete is Asian and "wears ties"—whatever that means. He's trendy. I've heard from other people that he thinks he's a DJ. Another girl who knows him says he can be snotty at times but she also said he is hilarious.*

DAMIEN LOEB. *Goes to the Multnomah Learning Center downtown (your favorite school, Chloe).*

Looks pretty normal, and pretty clean-cut by MLC standards. Is an insane blogger, LiveJournal guy. Once wrote continuously for 32 hours. You can read his journals if you want. He gets fan mail from all over the world for his outrageous opinions. Has a little computer genius disease, has trouble dealing with actual people.

JUSTIN CLEMENTE. *Supposedly super cute. Unfortunately he's a male cheerleader and is probably gay (according to many people). Several girl cheerleaders liked him and he did nothing about it. Sorry, Chloe, no gay guys for you. I know you like them, but this is PROM—you have to try for love! However, if you don't like anyone else, we can ask him.*

TWO WILD CARDS:

JIM SHAW. *The "foam hat guy." Junior. Goes to Lincoln downtown. Wears his pants off his ass and never shampoos his hair. Too cool for school and "a serious asshole" if he doesn't like you, according to one person. BUT he dated the super sweet Mandy Walsh, who everyone loves and who shocked all of Lincoln when she went for him, so there must be something good about him.*

ROBERT LONGO. *Goes to Sunset. A very popular jock guy. Smart, though, and charming. His sister said he broke up with his girlfriend two weeks ago. He is one of the most popular people at his school and probably out of our league—but if you're feeling brave and want to call him, his sister said he might say yes.*

Chloe finished the list and began again at the top.

"Wow," Jace said to Laura. "You really did your homework."

"None of them are for sure," said Laura. "These are just possibilities." She turned the paper sideways so she could look at it with Chloe. "Also, we can Google them. We could even go find them if you want to."

"You want me to meet them?" asked Chloe.

"Not all of them. But if you like one or two, we could probably figure out a way to at least see them."

Chloe slid the paper back to Laura. "I can't choose. You have to choose."

"*Chlo*-e," said Laura. "At least tell me which ones you *kind of* like."

Chloe looked at the paper again. She studied it. "I kind of like the asshole. But that's why you have to choose."

"Really? Jim Shaw?"

Chloe shrugged. "I don't know. You've been to proms. You know what's the best kind of guy."

"The best kind of guy is whoever you like," said Jace helpfully.

"Why do I have to decide?" said Chloe. "Let them decide. They're the boys." Chloe pushed the paper away. "Isn't the boy supposed to ask the girl?"

"Of course the boy is supposed to ask the girl," said Laura. "Unfortunately, we're a little past that schedule-wise."

"This is why prom is so much work," added Jace. "It can be a very complicated process."

"We can't really wait for the guys," said Laura. "We have to act. And soon."

"This is too hard," said Chloe. She sat back and sighed. "Maybe this whole thing is a bad idea."

"Don't say that," said Laura. "We'll figure it out."

Jace smiled and agreed wholeheartedly. She didn't mention the looming problem that she didn't have a date yet, either.

11

That night Jace watched basketball with her father and three brothers. The NBA playoffs had begun, and as usual, her entire family was glued to the TV, cheering on their favorite team, the Dallas Mavericks. The Mavericks were huge in the Torres household, mainly because they had

Eduardo Najera, who was from Chihuahua, Mexico, about fifty miles from where her dad grew up.

Jace, who normally loved watching basketball, had trouble focusing. She kept thinking about Paul. Had he really turned down a girl in his history class? And who was it? And was his reason for saying no really because he had no history at Evergreen? Maybe he was just saying that because he liked someone else. But who?

Jace found herself running through the Year of Paul in her head. He had arrived in October, a disastrous time to arrive at a new school, especially junior year. Jace remembered the first time she saw him: at his locker, alone, befuddled, and yet somehow poised. With his slick blond hair, his Vans deck shoes, he looked very "California," which didn't help him fit in. She remembered hearing a rumor that he'd had family problems and had been forced to move up to Oregon with his aunt and uncle.

His first month was brutal. No friends. No one to talk to. Eating lunch alone, day after day, in Evergreen's overwhelming cafeteria. Jace, who had noticed him from the start, kept tabs on him, cautiously saying hi in the halls occasionally. To her classmates' credit, no one picked on him or harassed him in any way. They ignored him. They had their own friends, their own cliques. It was junior year; people were busy.

Then, in March, tennis tryouts began. On the first day, a new student beat Doug Rotter, who was Evergreen's best tennis player ever. This sent shock waves through the small Evergreen tennis community, and on the second day of tryouts, all the girl players hurried to the boys' courts to see who the new guy was. When Jace saw that it was Paul, the loner blond kid, she felt something happen in her chest. It was as if she recognized him from a dream or a distant memory. It was like she had been waiting for him her whole life.

Once he beat Doug Rotter, Paul became less invisible. Boys invited him places, girls tried to flirt with him. But there was something a tiny bit *off* about Paul; he was shy and evasive and slow to make friends. In the end, the girls found other boys to crush on.

Jace, though, found him irresistible. And not just because he was so cute. He seemed to need her. They seemed to fit together. She began by asking him questions about tennis, which was natural enough—she was a jock herself and she knew how to talk sports. He, in turn, asked her about the school: which teachers to avoid, where to sit at lunch, the inner workings of the important cliques. At first Jace had assumed he would ditch her eventually and conquer Evergreen's social scene as effortlessly as he had the tennis team. Instead he listened and observed and remained distant. He was very shy. Or maybe it was the problems with his family.

Then the tennis season began. They began sitting together in the van. They hung out between matches. He had even called her a couple times. It seemed like something was happening, but what? For the first time in her life, Jace hated being such a tomboy. She wanted to know about boys. How did you read them? How could you tell what they were thinking? She had never given them much notice before. And now she was paying for it.

12

At school the next day, Betsy appeared at Jace's locker. "I just saw Paul going into the library," she whispered. "By himself."

"So?"

"So? This is your chance. Go ask him to the prom."

"Betsy," whispered Jace. "I already asked him at the Glencoe match. He wouldn't answer."

"Did you *really* ask him or did you hint?" asked Betsy.

"I hinted. And I asked. Sort of. The point is, he doesn't like me like that."

"I don't believe it," said Betsy. "You have to ask him straight-up. All you've done is drop hints. Guys don't understand hints. You have to ask him. You have to say: 'Paul, will you go to the prom with me?'"

Jace looked at her.

"I think he'll say yes. I really do. And I'm your tennis partner; I wouldn't lie to you."

Jace walked to the library. She couldn't help a desperate here-we-go-again feeling as she approached it. She watched her fellow students going in the other direction. What were these people doing about prom? They didn't look worried. They didn't seem to have a care in the world.

At the library, she opened the door and went in. Betsy was right. The only way was to ask him point-blank. Something like, *Listen, Paul, I know I haven't been up-front about this, but the fact is . . .*

But that sounded too apologetic. She could still be casual, even as she was being direct: *Hey, Paul, what's up, you know there's this thing I've been meaning to ask you. . . .*

No, that sounded too sneaky. She needed to sound serious: *Paul, I want to go to the prom with you, I know what you're thinking, you don't really like me like that, but could you do it as a favor? . . .*

No. Too needy. It needed to be more like, *Paul, I know we've been mostly tennis friends but I think it's time to take things to the next level.* But she hated that "next level" phrase. That was big at Evergreen lately; everyone was always taking things to the "next level."

No, she would just have to look him square in the eye and blurt it out.

She stopped. Paul was sitting on one of the couches in the back. Beside him was Jessica Nielsen—Jessica who was totally hot and notorious for hooking up with cute jocks. Jace stood and watched. Paul was telling her a story. Jessica listened, laughed, smiled at him. Paul sliced his hand through the air like an airplane or a skateboard crashing. Jessica laughed in that fake loud way that could only mean one thing.

She had asked him to the prom. Could it be? Did Jessica have a date? Did she have a current boyfriend? Jace didn't know. She would have to ask Laura. Why didn't Jace know these things herself? Why didn't she pay attention? Why was she such an idiot? And worst of all: WHY HAD SHE WAITED SO LONG TO ASK PAUL!?

Jace ran for the safety of the cafeteria. She found Betsy and collapsed beside her. "I blew it. I'm too late," she said. "You have to help me, Betsy. I have to get another prom date. Laura is going to kill me."

"Paul said no?"

"He didn't have to say no. He was already saying yes to Jessica Nielsen!"

"Jessica Nielsen?" said another girl. "But I thought—"

Jace, in her distress, did not let her finish. "They were in the library!" she cried. "Together! She was laughing at his jokes!"

"Oh wait," said Betsy, watching the cafeteria entrance. "Here comes Paul now."

"Oh my God," moaned Jace. "I'm so embarrassed. If he goes with her . . ." She lowered her head, which unfortunately dropped the ends of her black hair into Betsy's peach cobbler. Betsy, seeing this, tried to brush Jace's hair away but only managed to move it into the mashed potatoes and gravy.

"There you are," said Paul. Jace lifted her head and looked up. Paul smiled nervously. Then he pointed. "You, uh . . ." he said. "You got some . . . in your hair. . . ."

Jace saw the mashed potatoes in her hair. Betsy quickly grabbed a napkin and wiped it away. Jace helped, frantically.

"Uh," said Paul, when the gravy was gone, "could I talk to you for a second?"

Jace sat, in shock, staring up into Paul's face.

Betsy nudged her under the table.

"Oh," said Jace. "Sure." She stood. She walked with Paul away from the table.

"I wanted to ask you something. . . ." started Paul.

"Yes?" said Jace, her eyes brightening.

"If you'd like to . . . uh . . ." said Paul, nervously.

Jace's face flushed with excitement. Her heart began to soar. Her whole body seemed to float for a moment.

Paul continued: "See there's this . . . this sports banquet thing, the newspaper puts on . . . for boys' spring sports. . . ."

Jace felt her heart collapse. Her chest was suddenly full of lead.

"It'll probably be boring and way too crowded . . ." said Paul. "But they said I could bring a friend, and if you felt like it. "

"Oh," said Jace, the color draining out of her face.

"Do you think you'd want to?"

Jace stared at him blankly. "Sure," she said.

"You don't look too psyched."

"No, I'll go," said Jace, without enthusiasm.

Paul smiled with relief. "Good. I'm glad. I kinda feel like you've been avoiding me lately. Like you don't want to talk to me."

Jace stared at him.

"'Cause I miss it when we don't talk," said Paul. "I mean, I know you have a lot going on right now."

"I don't have that much *going on*," said Jace. "Trust me."

"Well," said Paul. "As long as everything's cool."

"What about Jessica?" said Jace, swallowing.

"What about her?"

"Are you friends with her now?"

Paul gave Jace a puzzled look. "I guess so. She likes Doug Rotter. I think they're going to the prom."

"They are?" said Jace.

"Yeah," said Paul. "What about you? Did you ever decide what you're doing about that?"

"No," said Jace. "I never did."

"You don't have much time," said Paul, without looking at her. "You better figure it out."

"Yeah," said Jace. "I guess I better."

13

Laura Truman stared blankly into the mall concourse from the Staples customer service counter. It had been a long, slow day, and she had a lot on her mind.

Abby Maxwell appeared. She worked at Girl Talk, the trendy clothing store on the other end of the mall. "Laura," said Abby. "Hey! Earth to Laura!"

Laura lifted her head and smiled politely. Abby was also a junior at Evergreen, though she and Laura were not really friends. Abby seemed to think they would be, now that they worked at the mall together. Laura was not so sure. Abby wore miniskirts and fishnets and lots of make-up. She had slept with one of the punk boys from Muzik Express and bragged about it to everyone. She wasn't exactly Laura's type.

"How's the Chloe Thomas date search?" asked Abby.

"Nothing so far," said Laura. Despite Laura's misgivings about her, Abby had produced some of the better suggestions for Chloe's prom date. "How about you? Any new ideas?" asked Laura.

"I might have something, actually," said Abby. "My boyfriend, Eric, has this goofy friend who goes to Glencoe. I could give him a call."

"Anything would help at this point."

Abby smiled. "How's Staples?"

"Okay."

"How's Mike?"

"Fine," said Laura. She didn't appreciate someone like Abby asking her personal questions about her love life. Abby obviously did not take these things as seriously as Laura did.

"You seem a little spaced-out," said Abby, with genuine concern.

"No," said Laura, sitting up. "I was just thinking about stuff."

"All right," said Abby, pleasantly. "Well I gotta get home. I'll try Eric's friend and let you know."

"Okay," said Laura. "Thanks."

It was now after seven; the mall was nearly empty. Laura did a slow walk around Staples, picking up trash, straightening inventory.

Then she heard a familiar sound: paper getting stuck in the copy machine. Laura didn't understand why they bothered to keep the copy machine. All it did was jam. And get ink all over the employees. She walked over and found a boy standing beside it. He was reading a book, unaware that his copies were being mangled.

"Hey," said Laura. "Your copies are bunching up."

The boy looked but didn't know what to do. Laura yanked out the crooked bottom sheet and left the machine running. The copies were on colored paper. They were flyers for Westview, the newest high school in Evergreen's district. "Oh," said Laura as she read one of them. "You go to Westview?"

The boy nodded nervously. "Yeah, these are for a dance we're having," he said. "I'm kinda on the student council. Our printer broke."

"Oh," said Laura, suddenly nervous herself. She didn't know why she would be. She helped people all day. She looked down at the poster. Across the top was written, "I KNOW YOU WANT TO HIT THAT!"

"You're having a dance this late in the year?" asked Laura. "Don't you have a prom?"

"Yeah, but only juniors and seniors go. This is for the sophomores and frosh."

"Oh," said Laura. Somewhere in her brain the idea formed that she should talk to this boy. He was cute. He was nice. He was on the student council. Maybe Chloe would like him. "Uh, can I ask you something?"

"Sure," said the boy.

But Laura's brain couldn't figure out how to ask the question. And what was the question? Who are you? Why do I feel the need to talk to you? Instead she said, "Is that a French book?"

The book in his hands had a picture of Europe on the cover. "No, this is European history. After World War Two. It's AP."

"Oh," said Laura. Now her brain went completely

blank. She was speechless. She never lost her cool like this. It must have been the stress of everything going on.

"My name's Ryan by the way," said the boy. He was nervous, too, but he was happy-nervous. He grinned and shuffled his feet in a nerdy way. "I go to Westview. Where do you go?"

"Evergreen," said Laura. "I work here nights."

"Yeah?" he said. "I work part-time at Happy Pet upstairs. Only two nights a week, though."

"That's nice," said Laura, a little too sharply. She tried to think of something else to say but she couldn't. "I should probably get back," she said.

"Sure," said Ryan. "What's your name?"

"Laura."

"Oh, okay. Well thanks for saving my posters."

"You won't have to pay for these," Laura said, grabbing the mangled sheets. She did this not to save him the money but as an excuse to stand there one second longer. When she straightened up, she stared directly into his smiling face. *What was it about him?* Then she regained her composure and walked curtly back to the customer service counter.

When he was gone, Laura picked up the phone and called Chloe at home.

"It's me," said Laura. "I need to talk to you."

"Sure," said Chloe. "What's up?"

Laura took a breath. "I feel like you're not trying very hard on the prom thing," she said.

Chloe went silent.

"I feel like you're not putting very much effort into finding a date," said Laura.

Chloe wasn't sure how to respond. "Okay," she said.

"What do you think?" said Laura.

"I sort of thought you wanted to do it."

"I do but I feel like . . . like right now a boy came into the store." She turned and looked down the concourse as she said this. "He came in and I tried to talk to him, you know, for your sake but I got all nervous. I was sweating. And he seemed perfect. He had a book about Europe."

"Yeah?" said Chloe.

"And he was, like, really sweet and really . . . I don't know. It doesn't seem fair."

"What doesn't?"

"Just . . . I don't know."

"Who was he?"

"His name is Ryan. He goes to Westview. He had the nicest face. . . . He seemed . . . He was smart. He was on the student council. But I didn't get his number."

"Why not?"

"*Because.* I have a boyfriend! I can't ask boys for their number!"

Chloe sat on her bed and wondered what was going on with her friend. She sometimes worried about Laura.

There were rumors about Mike around school. Rumors about him and other girls.

"I'll help more if you want," said Chloe. "But you're so much better at that stuff."

"It doesn't matter," said Laura. The anger had drained out of her. Now she was just there, on the line.

"Laura?" said Chloe.

"Yeah?"

"Are you all right?"

"Yeah, I'm a little stressed," admitted Laura.

"Where's Mike?"

"I don't know. He had baseball practice. I think he's with Daniel and those guys."

Chloe waited for her to say more.

"It's just . . . I get tired of trying so hard all the time," said Laura. "I want Mike to try sometimes."

"Yeah," said Chloe. "That makes sense."

Laura steadied herself. "So if that guy comes back should I try to get his number?"

"Sure, if you want to."

"I think he might be a good person. There was something about him. He was so . . . not full of himself."

"Sounds like he really made an impression on you," said Chloe.

"Yeah. But not for me. For you. I mean—oh God. I don't know what I mean, my hands are shaking."

"Don't worry," said Chloe. "And if he comes back, get his number. Do it for me."

"Okay. I will."

"Laura, can I say something?"

"What?"

"Mike doesn't own you. You can talk to other people."

"I know that," said Laura.

"And Mike is a senior. He's not going to be here next year. At some point . . ."

"Actually, I have to go," said Laura, suddenly. "We're starting cleanup. The other people want to get home."

"Okay."

14

"Are you sure this is the right way?" Chloe asked Shawnie, as they walked through a dark alley in the depths of downtown Portland. They were going to see a band with some of Shawnie's punk friends.

"Of course I'm sure," said Shawnie. "I come here all the time."

It was a damp, foggy night. Chloe stepped over an oily puddle. She didn't like going downtown. She was afraid of Shawnie's friends and she hadn't even met them yet.

"Don't worry," Shawnie assured her. "It's an all-ages place. It's for kids."

"Yeah, but what kind of kids?" said Chloe.

"Listen, if you can give the prom a chance, you can give this a chance," said Shawnie.

They found the entrance and went inside. It was a big empty space. There were a few chairs and a stage and, as Shawnie had promised, several small packs of teenagers scattered around the room. They all looked tough and unapproachable. "When's Rebecca coming?" Chloe asked.

"She'll be here, relax," said Shawnie. "Hey, there's Crystal!"

They approached a group of girls standing in the back. The girls were dressed downtown-style. Crystal wore tons of black eye makeup and a tie over a T-shirt that said "Star Effer" on it. When Chloe was introduced to her, Crystal looked her up and down like a piece of meat.

"Chloe's going to the prom," Shawnie told the girls. They all scoffed.

All except Crystal. "I went to my prom last year," she said loudly.

"You did?" said Shawnie, surprised. "Was it horrible?"

"Not at all," said Crystal.

The other girls pressed closer to hear about it.

"I took two hits of Ecstasy," bragged Crystal. "And made out with a bunch of people in the back of a limo."

"With *a bunch* of people?" asked Chloe.

"Sure," said Crystal. "My date and his ex-girlfriend, and this other girl. And this other guy we picked up."

"Why did you do that?" asked Chloe.

"Why?" laughed Crystal. "Because I felt like it. I love grouping on E. Especially when there's lots of girls involved. Then the boys get all nervous."

The other girls laughed. Shawnie loudest of all. Chloe tried to smile and not look too embarrassed.

Shawnie and Chloe stood with Crystal and her friends while the first band played. Then Rebecca arrived. Chloe was greatly relieved to see her. The two of them retreated to the bathroom.

"Don't let Shawnie try to shock you with her friends," Rebecca advised. "She loves to do that."

"That Crystal is scary."

"She's not, though, it's just an act. Her dad writes Christian self-help books. We don't have to hang out with them. We can go to the front of the stage. That's the funnest, anyway."

"How do you know so much about this?" said Chloe.

Rebecca shrugged. "Hanging out with Shawnie, I guess."

They watched the next band from the very front of the stage. They were called The Vexers. The lead singer was short, and strutted around, taunting the audience and striking outrageous poses.

Chloe had never seen anything like it. She got water splashed on her by the drummer. She helped catch the singer when he threw himself into the audience. It was totally fun.

Near the end of the show, Rebecca tapped Chloe on the shoulder and pointed to two guys standing behind them. They were cute and obviously in high school. The taller one said something to Rebecca. It was hard to hear. He shouted it: "What does your button say?"

Rebecca looked down at the button on her coat. " 'Girls kick ass,' " she shouted back.

The guy nodded. "Where do you guys go?"

"Evergreen. Where do you go?"

"Lincoln."

Rebecca nodded. The next song started. The guys stood behind them and nodded their heads to the music. Chloe and Rebecca nodded their heads too, but not too much. The Vexers singer took a big sip of water and spat it onto the crowd.

Afterward, people stood around on the sidewalk outside. Crystal and Shawnie disappeared, and Rebecca offered Chloe a ride home. Then the two boys showed up. "Hey, what are you guys doing?" the tall one asked.

"Going home," said Rebecca.

"Wanna give us a ride to Northwest?"

"Sure."

The two boys sat in back. They talked about the show, about The Vexers, about another show the next weekend.

The taller boy, Josh, said, "We're having a party tomorrow night. You guys should come by."

"Yeah?" said Rebecca.

"I'll give you the address. You got something to write on?"

Chloe got a pen out of the glove box and wrote it down. The boys got out in Northwest and thanked them for the ride. Josh leaned down to the passenger window. "What was your name again?"

"I'm Chloe," said Chloe. "And she's Rebecca."

"All right," said Josh. "Nice to meet you guys. Come to our party."

"Okay," said Chloe.

15

The next morning, Chloe woke up restless and excited. She got up, ate breakfast, and went to Barnes & Noble. It was crowded on a Saturday, but the world history section was empty. It always was.

Chloe was there at ten thirty. Rebecca showed up at eleven. They took their usual places. The sharp caffeine tang of Starbucks wafted through the store. Chloe lay on her stomach and tried to write a poem about the night before. It was mostly about Crystal and how pretentious yet fascinating she was.

"Maybe you could invite one of those Lincoln boys to the prom," suggested Rebecca.

"Which one would I ask?"

"The tall one, Josh," said Rebecca. "He's the one who talked to you."

"He didn't talk to me like *that*."

"He kinda did. He asked you your name."

"He was being polite," said Chloe, doodling on her notepad.

"Do you think he'd go with you?" asked Rebecca.

"I doubt it," said Chloe. "And I'd have to check with Laura."

"Maybe I should invite someone," said Rebecca.

Chloe looked up with surprise. "To the prom?"

"Why not?" said Rebecca. "Or would that be too weird? Probably no one would want me there."

"People wouldn't care," said Chloe. "You could go; you totally could. I didn't think you wanted to."

"I guess I don't. And who would go with me?"

"Maybe those Lincoln boys," said Chloe. "You said so yourself. They invited us to their party."

"Yeah, but they probably invited lots of girls."

Chloe continued to doodle. Then she set down her pen. "Let me use your cell phone."

Chloe called Laura at Staples. "Hey," she said. "I think I found someone for the prom."

"You did?" said Laura. "Is it someone from the list?"

"No, it's a guy I met. He's cute, though. He goes to Lincoln."

"Where did you meet him?"

"At this place downtown that Shawnie took me to. A punk show."

"Do you know him well?" asked Laura.

"No. I just met him."

"That's not the best way to do it, Chloe."

"But he's cute, and Rebecca thinks he likes me."

"But we don't know anything about him," reasoned Laura. "We know things about the people on the list. We have friends who are friends with them."

"But *I* don't know them."

"That's not crucially important. What's important is that they're the right kind of person for a prom. Do you understand? A guy from a punk show probably isn't."

"He wasn't punk himself."

"Chloe," said Laura, with some impatience, "prom is not only about you and your date. It's about the whole experience. Jace and I have to go with this person, too. What if he gets drunk or throws up or something?"

"Isn't that what everyone does?"

"No, Chloe. Jeez."

"So you think I should only go with someone off the list?"

"Listen, I made some calls yesterday. We still have some very good possibilities. I really think that's the best way to do it. It's more appropriate."

Chloe hated the word *appropriate*. It made her cringe to hear it. But she didn't feel like arguing with Laura. "All right," she said. She handed the phone back to Rebecca.

"What did she say?" said Rebecca.

"She says it's not cool to ask some guy off the street."

"Well that's easy for her to say, since she's had a boyfriend forever."

• • •

Rebecca and Chloe had only become friends that year, so when Chloe went to Rebecca's before the Lincoln party, it was her first time inside the Anderson house. Rebecca's parents weren't as cultural as Chloe's. They didn't have organic bread or bookshelves or posters from the Portland Art Museum. They had a four-foot-wide TV and a NASCAR calendar on their refrigerator.

"I can't believe we're going to this party," Chloe said, sitting on Rebecca's bed.

"I know," said Rebecca. "Me neither."

"Have you ever been invited to something by a stranger like that?" asked Chloe.

"No."

"Maybe we shouldn't even go."

"I think we better," said Rebecca. "It might never happen again."

"Yeah," said Chloe. "I guess so."

At eight thirty they went to the party. Josh's house was nestled in the hills of Weston Heights. It looked small from outside, but inside it was beautiful and fancy and had a view of the entire city. Unfortunately there was no one there yet.

"Look at this place," whispered Chloe. She was wearing a badly fitting Salvation Army dress and her red plastic barrette, which parted her hair to the side.

"His parents must be rich," said Rebecca, curling her

fists up in the sleeves of her oversized military coat. She wore her "Girls Kick Ass" button prominently. She thought better of it now and put it in her pocket.

"The Lincoln girls are going to be totally hot," said Chloe.

"We're too early, though," said Rebecca. "Maybe we should leave and come back."

"No, we'll never come back. We better stay."

Rebecca agreed. They ventured farther into the house, past the kitchen and the large sunken living room. There was a wood deck outside. The glass doors were open. They went outside and gazed down at the city below. Two lounge chairs faced the view.

"Let's sit out here for a while," said Chloe.

"I'll get us some drinks," said Rebecca.

"We'll act like we own the place," said Chloe, taking a seat. Rebecca disappeared inside and was back a minute later. She handed Chloe a tall glass of yellow liquid. "What's this?" asked Chloe.

"A screwdriver."

Chloe tasted it. It was so strong it burned her lips. "Ewww!"

Rebecca settled herself next to Chloe. "Okay," said Rebecca. "We'll act like we own the place."

"Okay, starting now, we own the place," said Chloe.

Rebecca tried her drink. "Oh my gawd!" she said, touching her mouth. "That's terrible."

"What did you put in it?"

"Vodka and orange juice," said Rebecca. "Isn't that right?"

"I guess so," said Chloe. "But it's supposed to be mostly orange juice."

"I thought it was supposed to be half and half," said Rebecca, trying it again.

"Just drink it," said Chloe, forcing down a tiny sip. "We'll need it. It'll help if we have to talk to people."

16

Meanwhile, at her own house, Jace was waiting for Paul to pick her up for the sports banquet. She was pretending to watch the Mavericks playoff game with her dad and brothers, though she could barely follow what was happening. When she heard the faint rumble of a car pulling into the driveway, she snuck out of the room and ran to the front hallway. She opened the front door before Paul could ring the bell.

"Oh," said Paul, surprised to be met so promptly.

"Shhh," said Jace.

"Who's here?" called her father from the TV room.

"Just someone from the tennis team, Dad."

"Where are you going?"

"We're going to the banquet," she yelled. "The thing I told you about."

"In by twelve!"

"Dad," she yelled back. "My curfew is one!"

"All right, twelve thirty then," said her father. "Who are you going with?"

"Nobody. Some tennis people."

"Is it a boy?" he said, threatening to come investigate.

"It's just Paul, from the tennis team," she repeated. "Bye!" She pushed Paul out the door. "Gawd, can you believe him?"

In the driveway they walked to Paul's red Volkswagen convertible. Paul opened Jace's car door for her. He took his own seat without speaking and started the engine. It all felt a little stiff and formal to Jace.

Paul drove. Jace watched her neighborhood float by outside her window.

"I hope it's not too crowded," said Paul. He seemed anxious about it.

"If it's a banquet, it probably will be," said Jace. "At least it's not football season."

"I don't like big social things," said Paul, shifting. "I get weird if there's too many people around."

"Really?" said Jace, watching him. "Like how?"

"I get anxious and stuff. I have this thing."

"Yeah? What thing?"

"It's nothing. It's this . . . condition. It's called *agoraphobia.*" He shifted again. He was driving very fast. "Basically, if you're in a really crowded room or someplace where there's a lot of people, you freak out."

"What happens?" asked Jace.

"Nothing really. Panic attacks."

Jace had never heard of such a thing. "Do you go to a doctor for it?"

"Yeah, they have meds for it."

"Really, you take pills? For that?"

Paul nodded. He looked at her. "Actually, I don't usually tell people about the meds, so . . ."

"No, no, I won't tell anyone."

"It's pretty common, actually," said Paul, slowing down for a stop sign. "Lots of people have it."

Jace nodded her agreement, though she certainly didn't know anyone who had panic attacks or took "meds" or went to doctors for things like that. Maybe it was something people did in California. They were more into psychological issues down there.

The banquet was at an Elks Lodge in downtown Beaverton. They parked in the gravel lot. Inside, they found themselves in a huge, noisy room packed with people. Jace could feel Paul hesitate at the sight of it. A man approached Paul, shook his hand, and welcomed him. A woman gave Paul a name-tag sticker that said: "Paul Stoyanovich, Evergreen Tennis." Paul reluctantly stuck it to his shirt.

The two made their way to their assigned table. Doug Rotter and Jessica Nielsen were already there. Doug had his name tag on. Other people were milling around, athletes, parents, friends. Paul and Jace took their seats.

"Hey! Paul Stoyanovich!" said a red-haired boy, suddenly slapping Paul on the back. "Remember me? I played you in the California Regionals a couple years ago."

"Yeah?" said Paul, looking up from his chair.

"You smoked my ass. What are you doing up here?" joked the boy. "Not playing tennis I hope!"

Paul laughed politely. The boy said something else but it was hard to hear in the loud room. The boy ran off and Paul looked around the room. Every seat was taken and people were jammed along the walls. There were video cameras. In the front was a long table and a spotlit podium where people were preparing to speak.

"Do *we* have to go up there?" Paul asked Doug.

"I think so," answered Doug.

"Christ," said Paul. Jace could see the tension in his face. He looked very anxious.

Jace scooted her chair closer to him. "Are you okay?"

"Yeah," said Paul, wiping his forehead with a napkin.

"Hey, whatever happened to you, anyway?" said the red-haired boy. He was back. "You were, like, number two in fourteen-and-unders. Did you move or something?"

"Yeah, kinda," said Paul, politely.

"What are you ranked up here? You should be number one. Coming from California and all."

Paul tried to smile. "Not that high. Fifteen, I think."

"Fifteen?" said the red-haired boy. "Is that all? Bro, what happened?"

"Excuse me. Excuse me," said a man at the podium.

"We're going to be get started soon. If people could get settled . . ."

The boy disappeared, but the damage was done. Paul was sweating. His knee was bouncing nervously under the table. "Do they have water here?" Paul asked Doug.

"Ask the waitress," said Jessica helpfully. "If she ever comes back."

Paul looked for the waitress. When he turned toward Jace, she suddenly understood what he'd been talking about in the car. There was a panic in his eyes she had never seen in a person before. It was worse than panic. It was a kind of terror.

"I'll get you some," said Jace, putting her hand firmly on his. She stood and pushed her way toward the kitchen. It took some pleading but she managed to get a red plastic glass full of tap water from the kitchen workers. She fought her way back to the table.

But Paul's chair was empty.

"Where's Paul?" she asked Doug.

"I don't know," said Doug, who was facing the stage.

"He was here a second ago," said Jessica.

"He better get back," said Doug. "Tennis is first this year. We gotta go up there."

17

"You guys, check out the view!" said a bouncy blonde girl at the Lincoln party. Chloe and Rebecca had been outside for over an hour, and only now were people beginning to show up. Chloe and Rebecca maintained their places on the lounge chairs. They were on their second screwdrivers, which they sipped in silence. As more Lincoln people appeared, they found themselves afraid to move.

"My drink's almost gone," whispered Chloe, as two particularly gorgeous Lincoln girls stood in front of them.

"Go get us some more," said Rebecca.

"Why do I have to go?"

"Because I got the last two."

Chloe sat for several minutes more. But her drink was now completely gone. She'd have to get up at some point. She sighed and got to her feet. That's when the alcohol hit her. She wobbled for a moment. "Whooooaaa," she said, almost falling over.

"Chloe!" hissed Rebecca.

"Shhhh," said Chloe. "I'm fine." She steadied herself and went inside. There were more people now. In the kitchen, Chloe looked for the vodka and almost got hit by two girls smashing ice with a hammer. Then a loud gang of cute boys came crashing into the kitchen. They were doing tequila shots. They stuck one in Chloe's hand and made her drink it. Chloe spilled most of it in the jostling, then choked down the rest.

When they left, she continued her search. The hard liquor was gone, so she grabbed two beers from the fridge. Heading back to the deck, she crossed the living room, where she saw Josh, surrounded by girls at the stereo. He happened to look up, and his eyes met Chloe's. She waved to him. And he waved back.

Outside, Chloe handed Rebecca her beer. "Oh my God," she whispered. "Josh just waved to me!"

"Really?" said Rebecca.

"I think I should ask him, don't you?" said Chloe, drinking her beer.

"What about what Laura said?" said Rebecca.

"She's too uptight," said Chloe, wobbling slightly on her feet. "I mean, who cares? It's my prom. Right?"

"Yeah but you wouldn't even be going if those guys didn't make you."

"They dint *make* me," said Chloe, drinking more beer. The alcohol was really hitting her now. "I got an idea. . . . Why don' I ask Josh and you ass his friend?"

"No way," said Rebecca. "I could never ask anyone to the prom."

"Why not? We could be a foursome."

"You're going with Laura and Jace. They're not going to want me."

"I'd rather go with you than Laura," said Chloe, burping. She was startled when she heard herself say that. "I mean, I like her and all," she said. "She's one a my ollest friends." She couldn't think of what else to say. She burped again. Her mouth had gone numb. "Becca?" she said.

"Yeah?"

"I think I'm drunk."

"Good. You need the practice. Everyone'll be drunk at the prom."

The party continued to grow. A steady stream of people came onto the wood deck to see the view. Most of them ignored the two girls sitting in the lounge chairs, even as they stood beside them. Chloe sat in silence. Rebecca pulled her military coat closer around her.

Then Josh appeared. He was calling someone on his cell phone. He wasn't getting through. He frowned and tried the number again.

"Hey," Chloe said to him.

"Hey," said Josh, not paying attention. He stood at the railing and listened to his phone. "You guys having fun?" he asked them, while he waited.

"*Yes*," giggled Chloe, trying to be coy.

Josh held up a finger. He left a message for whoever he had called. Then he hung up. For the first time he looked closely at the two girls. "Wait. You guys were at the Vexers show last night. What're your names again?"

Chloe told him her name. Then she decided to stand up. This was not as easy as it should have been. She lurched sideways, spilling her beer in the process. With a helping hand from Josh, she made it to her feet.

Since Chloe was upright, Rebecca felt obligated to stand also.

"So, Josh?" said Chloe, still trying for a cutesy, sexy tone of voice. "I wanted to ass you something."

"What?"

Rebecca reached over and tried to pull Chloe back.

It was no use. Chloe leaned drunkenly toward Josh. "Well, it's kinda . . . *perzonal*."

For a moment, Josh was interested. Chloe was okay-looking. And she had been at the punk show. Maybe she was one of those wild downtown chicks who'd fool around with you in the bathroom. He'd heard about girls like that.

"See, we have thiz thing at our school. You know *the prom*," said Chloe.

Josh frowned when he heard that.

Chloe didn't notice. "It's kinda a big deal," she said. She was having trouble expressing herself; her mouth had gone numb again.

"I know what a prom is," said Josh. "What about it?"

"Well, I don' have a date yet," slurred Chloe. "I mean, I'm definitely *going*. I tole my friends I would. They're sposed to figs me up with someone." This wasn't coming out right. Chloe struggled to find the clearest way to describe her situation. "So I still need a date or whatever. Someone, you know, to go with me and do the whole *prom* thing—"

Josh's mouth bent into a sneer. "You're asking me to your prom? I don't even know you."

"No, I know," mumbled Chloe. "But I'm prawlly not going to know my date anyway." Why was this sounding so wrong?

Rebecca took her friend's arm. "Chloe, this isn't a good time—"

"It's not that big a deal," said Chloe, loudly.

Josh glared at her. "I don't even know what school you go to."

"I go to Evergreen."

"Evergreen?" said Josh. "In Beaverton? I hate Beaverton."

Meanwhile, several other partygoers had overheard this conversation. "Oh my God," said a female voice behind Rebecca. "That loser girl just asked Josh to her prom."

"Which girl?" said another voice.

"That girl right there. With the ugly dress."

"She did!?"

"Yes. I heard her."

"Uhm, excuse me," a loud female voice said, interrupting Chloe. "Josh has a *girlfriend*? And she's actually *cute*? Unlike *you*?"

Chloe turned and found herself face-to-face with six

angry Lincoln girls. Behind them, several guys watched with beers in hand.

"Chloe, we should probably go, like *now*," whispered Rebecca.

"God, I hope you're drunk," a girl said to Chloe.

"Why are you at our party, anyway?" said another. "Why don't you go back to Beaverton."

"Yeah, go back to Skankerton."

"And leave our guys alone."

"Why would they even want you?"

Rebecca and Chloe absorbed this onslaught with blank faces. Then the girls attacked Rebecca.

"And who's this one?" said a girl.

"Check *her* out."

"Nice coat. What are you, in the army?"

"Maybe she's a lesbian."

"Maybe they're both lesbians!"

Rebecca took Chloe's elbow and began to guide her carefully around the gang of girls.

"And look at that hideous dress!"

"Nice barrette!"

"God, who dresses you people?"

"You're, like, white trash. And you don't even know it!"

Rebecca dragged Chloe forcibly down the driveway.

"Oh my God," said Chloe. "What just happened?"

"We just got our asses kicked," said Rebecca, who was furious, in her timid way.

They got in Rebecca's car. They sat. Chloe began to process the situation. "I can't believe I did that. I asked that guy out, and he totally rejected me."

"I know," muttered Rebecca. "I was there."

"And those girls . . ."

"Those girls kicked our ass," said Rebecca, checking behind the rearview mirror, to make sure the girls hadn't followed them.

"Oh my God," said Chloe, hiding her face in her hands. "And it's all my fault. I'm sorry. I'm so sorry."

"I should have known," said Rebecca, starting the car. "See what happens when you think you can go to the prom? When you think you can hang out with popular people? That's what happens. They cut you down to nothing."

18

Jace searched the crowded Elks Lodge for Paul. She tried the bar, the kitchen, the restrooms. Everywhere she went she had to fight through the people. Adults scowled at her. They told her to sit down. One man told her she'd be thrown out if she didn't take her seat.

Jace kept searching. When she couldn't find Paul inside, she pushed through the front doors and walked outside into the parking lot. It was quiet outside. Crickets chirped in the darkness. She moved along the rows of silent cars, the gravel crunching under her feet. There was no sign of Paul anywhere.

She tried his Volkswagen. It was at the end of the lot. She approached it from behind and peeked in; he was there. He sat motionless, his forehead resting against the top of the steering wheel. He looked like he'd been shot.

"Paul? Paul!" said Jace, knocking on the passenger window. "Are you all right?"

Embarrassed by his pose, he sat up and opened Jace's door. "Hey," he said, with fake cheerfulness.

Jace got inside. She closed her door. "What are you doing? Why are you out here?"

"I just needed some air."

"I tried to get you some water. . . ." Jace turned to him. "Why did you leave?"

Paul shook his head. "It's like I told you. I can't handle stuff like that."

"Because of your thing? The agra-whatever?"

"Yeah," he said. He gripped the steering wheel.

Jace caught her breath. "You could have said something. Is it really that bad?"

"It kinda is," said Paul. He turned away from her and thought for a moment. "To be honest, that's really just the tip of the iceberg."

Jace wondered what kind of iceberg would have panic attacks at its tip? Then she saw the clock on the dashboard. "Doug Rotter said you guys were going first."

"Yeah?" said Paul.

"We should probably go back, don't you think?"

"Actually, I don't think I'm going back."

"But you have to," said Jace. "All the tennis players have to stand on the stage. Coach Hawkins will have a fit."

Paul's head sunk forward until his forehead rested against the top of the steering wheel again. "Jace," he said. "There's something I have to tell you."

Jace stared at him in alarm. "What?"

"I've had some problems."

Jace's heart did something strange. It seemed to move in her chest. It seemed to move toward Paul. "What kind of problems?"

"Problems besides agoraphobia. Problems with other kinds of . . . mental illness."

"Oh," said Jace.

"I was in lockdown a year ago. I spent three months in a psych ward. It was, like, padded cells, the whole deal. I had to drop out of school. I had to drop everything. It was really bad."

"Oh," said Jace.

Paul took a deep breath. "One night I drove my car through a parking lot at, like, sixty and I hit a bunch of cars and I hurt an old woman. I almost killed her."

"Why'd you do that?" asked Jace.

Paul shook his head. "I thought people were chasing me."

"Were they?"

"No."

Jace watched Paul's eyes blink in the darkness.

"I could have gone to jail. But my dad's a lawyer, and he got me off."

"Oh," said Jace.

"Sorry to burden you, but I just . . . it just gets a little weird, you know, not being able to say anything . . . and trying to be Mr. Tennis and all that. I mean I have doctors to talk to, but it's not the same. . . ."

Jace listened to this. "Wow," she said. "I had no idea."

"That's the thing. I don't want to freak people out. But I get so tired of pretending . . . to be like everybody else. I just—" His head dipped lower. He closed his eyes.

Jace watched him.

"And you're, like . . . so awesome," said Paul. "And, like, the best friend I have at this school. But I feel so dishonest. Not telling you the truth. And feeling like my whole life is such a disaster."

"It's not, though," said Jace. "You're doing great. I mean, you beat Doug Rotter . . . and . . . and you're so nice. Everyone says that. You're the nicest guy I've ever met."

Paul's head was still down. Jace looked across the parking lot. "Oh no!" she said suddenly. "Here comes Coach Hawkins!"

Paul immediately sunk down in his seat.

"Stay down. I'll get rid of him," said Jace. She quietly opened her door, slipped out, and snuck away. Mr. Hawkins was walking through the cars by the front. Jace, crouching down, ran several cars in the opposite direction. When Mr. Hawkins turned away, she stood up and strolled casually toward him.

"Jace! There you are!" he said. "Where the hell is Paul?"

"He got sick," said Jace, which was sort of true. "He went home."

"He went home?" said Mr. Hawkins. "Is he crazy? He's supposed to be with the team. He's our number-one guy!"

Jace shrugged. "He was really sorry. He wanted to stay."

Coach Hawkins stared at her. "He left? He's really gone?"

She nodded.

Mr. Hawkins scratched his head. "All right. If you say so. Strange kid that one. Great tennis player, though." He turned and went back into the Elks Lodge.

Jace pretended to follow, then stopped, then backed up. When Mr. Hawkins was safely inside she ran back to the red Volkswagen.

"Oh my God!" she squealed, as she crawled back into the Volkswagen.

Paul rose up from his seat. "Is he gone?" said Paul.

"Yes, yes!" said Jace, giddily.

"Was he mad?"

"A little. Not too bad."

Paul sat up and started the car. "Let's get out of here!"

19

At ten A.M. on Sunday morning, Laura officially opened
Staples for business. She liked opening; she liked the still-
ness of the early hour, the hush of the gigantic mall concourse, empty and full of sunlight.

She opened the metal gate and swept up around the
front entrance. She found herself glancing up at the second level as she did. Petland was on the second level. She
had walked by it last night to see if Ryan was working. He
hadn't been. Should she go up there later? She wanted to,
mainly to question him more, to see if he was right for
Chloe. But also to see him. He had such a friendly face.
She wanted to look at it again.

"Hey!" asked Abby, who was arriving late, as usual,
for her own job at Girl Talk. "So have you found Chloe a
prom date?" she asked.

"No, not yet," said Laura, brushing her dirt into a neat
pile.

"Because I think I have someone."

"Yeah?" said Laura.

"That friend of Eric's. The one who goes to Glencoe."

Laura swept. "Glencoe guys are such hicks, though."

"He's not. His parents are starting an organic farm. They used to live downtown."

"Huh," said Laura.

"Zach Skinner is his name," continued Abby. "He's actually very cool. I bet Chloe would like him. He's kind of goofy. But he's smart, too."

Laura pushed her dirt into a pile. "Do you have his number?"

"Right here."

Back inside, Laura washed her hands. Her cell phone rang. She wasn't supposed to use her own phone at work, but the manager wasn't there yet.

"Hello?" she said.

"Laura," said a trembling voice. "It's me, Chloe."

"Hey, Chloe," said Laura.

"I just wanted to tell you. I'm not going to the prom."

"You're not?"

"I can't handle it," said Chloe. "I hate proms. I hate people. I hate all of it."

"All right," said Laura, putting her hand on her hip. "What happened? What did you do last night?"

Chloe sniffled. "We went to that party."

"What party?"

"The party of those Lincoln guys we met."

"And let me guess," said Laura. "You asked that guy

and something bad happened. I told you not to ask a random guy."

"They all laughed at me! A whole group of them! They were horrible. And that's what's going to happen at the prom!"

"Chloe, listen to me," said Laura. "Nothing bad is going to happen at the prom. We're all going to go. We'll all be together. You'll be safe. You'll be fine."

"But I don't even have anyone to go with!"

"There's always someone to go with. Okay? In fact, I just talked to Abby about someone."

"I don't care. I don't want to anymore. I can't. I was wrong to ever think I could."

"Chloe, listen. You don't only go for yourself. You go for other people. So that people can see all their friends. So that people can have a total experience."

"I'm sorry, Laura, it's too late. I can't. Really. I'm not going. That's it."

"But I already called the guy," lied Laura. Desperate times called for desperate measures.

"Which guy?"

"This guy Abby told me about. And he was into it."

"He was?"

"Yes. He said you sounded very . . . interesting."

"He did?"

"Do you want me to tell him no? After all we've been through?"

"Well . . ."

"Chloe," said Laura. "I want you to forget about what happened at that party. Lots of stupid stuff happens at parties."

"Yeah."

"Let me talk to Zach again," said Laura. "And then we'll see where we are."

"That's his name? Zach?"

"That's right. And as soon as I confirm with him I'll call you. Is that all right? Do you trust me to handle this?"

"I don't know," sniffled Chloe. "I guess."

"You're going to the prom. And it's going to be one of the best nights of your life. Do you believe me?"

"Not really. But wait, his name is really Zach? I love that name."

"Let me call him. And I'll let you know."

20

Meanwhile, back at the Torres residence, Jace woke up early and gathered her tennis stuff. She walked down the street to the public tennis court and began whacking practice balls against the backboard. She hit them hard, as hard as she could. She was pissed this morning. She was mad at Paul. She was mad about the whole banquet situation. She had helped him. She had searched for him. She had lied to Coach Hawkins for him. And what did he do? He took her straight home and dropped her off, like nothing had happened.

Plus, *plus*, if he was going to confess all these things, the least he could do was talk to her about them, give her the rest of the story, answer her questions. Instead he took her straight home. It was almost like he'd become embarrassed. Or like now that she knew his secret, she was polluted, or unworthy, like now he didn't want her around anymore.

God, maybe he really was crazy. He sure didn't know how to deal with people. He sure didn't know how to treat his so-called friends.

She had been hitting balls for half an hour when the red Volkswagen pulled up.

Jace saw the car but ignored it. She saw Paul get out and take a seat on the little bench outside the tennis court. She continued to hit balls.

Finally he came onto the court. He stood behind her and watched her hit. "Jace?"

"Yeah?"

"I feel a little weird about last night," he said.

"Yeah?" she said, slamming a backhand. "So do I."

"What I told you. I probably shouldn't have said anything—"

"Why?" she said, without turning around. "Aren't I worthy of your secrets?"

Paul said nothing.

"I won't tell anyone," said Jace. "If that's what you're worried about."

"Why are you so pissed off?" said Paul.

"Why do you think?"

"I honestly don't know."

"I'm pissed off because . . ." She caught the ball in her hand. She stared back at him. "I'm pissed off because after you finally talk to me, finally open up to me for once, you just run off! And leave me hanging."

Paul squinted at her in the morning sunlight. "I'm sorry. I didn't realize."

"And what am I supposed to think?" continued Jace. "I'm lying in bed all night wondering: What just happened? Why did he tell me that? Is it because he likes me? Or is it because I was there?"

Paul didn't answer.

Jace turned back to the backboard and smacked her ball against it. "I'm also mad because I want to ask you to the prom and every time I get close to doing it, something happens. There's some problem or some situation and I can't ask you and I'm starting to feel like you do it on purpose."

"Wait," said Paul. "You want to ask *me* to the prom?"

"Of course I do. What do you think? Are you really that stupid?"

"I . . . I didn't know."

"And then you tell me all this stuff about you're crazy

and you've been in mental hospitals. And now I'm like, Do I *not* ask you? Do I ask you anyway? Do I give up on this whole thing? For all I know you're just saying these things to get rid of me."

"That's not true."

She turned and stared hard at him. "Well what am I supposed to think?"

"Not that."

Jace turned back to the backboard. "I don't know why I care so much about the stupid prom." She slammed the ball into the wall. "If you ask me, it's more trouble than it's worth."

"Jace?" said Paul.

"What?"

"If you want to go to the prom, I'll go."

Jace missed the ball. Or rather she let it go. It rolled past her, and Paul stopped it with his foot.

Jace turned to him. A sudden shyness came over her. "But how can you?" she asked. "What about your agrathing?"

"I think I can handle it."

Jace watched the ball at his feet. "But it'll be crowded. Probably worse than at the banquet."

"It's not so bad if I'm with other people. And if I'm not the center of attention."

Jace watched him.

He picked up the ball and threw it to her. She caught it. "So you'll go, just like that?" she murmured.

"Yes."

She looked at the ball. She looked at him.

Who *was* this boy?

21

Laura did not call Zach from Staples. She waited until she got home. She sat at her desk and consulted the original list of Chloe dates. She consulted the secondary lists. There were really no remaining options. Zach was her only hope. But under no circumstances should he suspect that.

She dialed the number Abby had given her. She rearranged her papers as the phone rang. "Hello?" said a boy.

"Zach? Hi. This is Laura Truman calling. I'm Abby Maxwell's friend?"

"Hey, what's up?"

"Not much," said Laura. "I wanted to ask you about our prom. At Evergreen."

"Oh yeah, Abby mentioned that. Someone needs a date?"

Laura cleared her throat. "Well, nobody *needs* anything. My friend Chloe is trying to choose which boy she wants to go with."

"Oh," said Zach.

"She doesn't really like any of the boys from our school. I mean, she likes them, but she wants to meet someone new, someone a little more interesting."

"Yeah?" said Zach. "Okay."

"She's a very unique person. She writes poetry. Do you know who Sylvia Plath is?"

"Uh . . . is she an actress?"

"No. She's a poet. She killed herself."

"Oh."

"So you don't read too much?" said Laura.

"No, I read," said Zach.

"What books do you like?"

"I dunno. *Harry Potter*?"

"Hmmm. What kind of movies do you like?"

"I liked *The Matrix*. The first one."

Laura wrote down "Harry Potter" and "Matrix" next to Zach's name. "What kind of music do you like?"

"Just whatever. Classic stuff. Metallica. Zeppelin."

Laura wrote that down. "What else can you tell me about yourself? Stuff that would make Chloe want to go with you."

"Like what sort of stuff?"

"I don't know. What's your favorite color?"

"My favorite color? Yellow?"

"Yellow?" said Laura.

"Or red maybe? I don't know."

Laura wrote this down. She hadn't intended to make this into a quiz. But it seemed to be working. "What do you look for in a girl?" she asked.

"Uhm . . ." said Zach. "Someone who's cool. And, you know, someone who's easy to talk to."

"Chloe is highly articulate," said Laura.

"What does that mean?"

"She's a good talker," said Laura. "If she thinks you're worth talking to. Her dad is a college professor. What do your parents do?"

"My parents . . . well . . . they're starting this organic farm. We just moved out here. It kinda smells. They use real cow manure and stuff. For fertilizer."

"Huh," said Laura.

"Listen," said Zach. "I'm not exactly an artistic genius or whatever. I just thought you needed someone to go to the prom."

"No, no, I'm only trying to . . . help Chloe make a decision."

"Abby's going with us, right? I mean, I only want to go if Abby and Eric are going."

"They are."

"'Cause I'd mainly be doing this for them. And I know if those guys are there, it won't totally suck."

"I can assure you the Evergreen prom isn't going to *suck*," said Laura. But she quietly wrote "loyal to friends" next to "Matrix" and "Yellow."

"No, I didn't mean that. . . ." said Zach.

"Let me check back with Chloe. Will you be home for a while?"

"Yeah."

"I'll call her and call you back."

Laura hung up and went downstairs. She made some microwave popcorn and watched the last half of *CSI: Miami* with her nana. Then she went back to her room. She called Zach.

"Chloe wants you to take her," Laura told Zach.

"Actually . . ." said Zach.

A surge of panic passed through Laura. "You still want to, right?"

"I guess. I just talked to Abby; she said Chloe's a little weird."

"She did?" said Laura, swallowing hard.

"But whatever. That's cool."

Laura sighed with relief. "So you'll go?"

"I'll go."

☑ DATES

☑ PREP

◯ PROM

22

Denny's was its usual greasy self when Chloe arrived for the second official prom meeting. Laura and Jace waited at a back booth. It was eight thirty, later than they would usually meet, but they had pressing business to discuss. They all had dates; they were all definitely going. Now it was time for preparations. And there was no time to lose. Prom was in ten days.

Before they could begin, the waitress appeared. They ordered their favorites. Jace had the cheeseburger deluxe; she was a jock, she could eat anything. Chloe ordered two eggs over easy; she liked to dip the corners of her toast in the yokes. Laura chose the grilled chicken salad. When the waitress was gone, Laura began her mini-lecture on pre-prom preparation: They should all get plenty of rest, they needed a slimming but nutritious diet, they should buy new underwear. . . .

But then a strange boy appeared. "Hey," he said, addressing Laura.

Laura looked up with annoyance, but her face changed instantly. It was Ryan. "Oh . . . hi," she said. "What are you doing here?"

"I always come here," he said. "It's where I do my homework. What are you guys doing?"

"We're uh . . . you know, talking girl stuff."

Ryan seemed more confident than he had at Staples. He smiled around at the three of them. "Girl stuff, huh?" he said.

"What's your homework?" asked Laura.

"AP chemistry. It blows."

"You must be smart," said Chloe.

"Nah, I just don't have anything better to do," said Ryan, glancing once at Laura.

Laura fell into an awkward silence.

"All right," said Ryan. "Well, I'm at the counter there. If you need a guy's opinion on anything."

"Okay," said Laura.

When he was gone. Jace leaned forward. "Who was *that*?" she said.

"Just some guy," said Laura. "He came into Staples once."

"Is that the guy you called me about?" Chloe asked.

"No," said Laura, flustered. "I mean, yes, yes it is, but you have a date now—"

"Whoever he is, he totally likes you," said Jace. "Does he know you have a boyfriend?"

"No," said Laura defensively. "Why would he? I only talked to him once."

"You better tell him," said Jace. "Oh my God, you're going to break his heart!"

"Stop it!" said Laura. "I told you. I barely know him."

"I noticed you didn't tell him about the prom," observed Chloe.

"Why should I?" said Laura.

"Oh my God, *you* like *him*!" whispered Jace.

"I do not!" said Laura. "Don't even say that!"

"It's weird to see a boy paying attention to you," said Chloe calmly. "No guys dare do that at school."

"Listen," said Laura, with force. "We have important things to discuss. Do you want to talk about some guy from the mall or do you want to talk about prom?"

Chloe and Jace backed off. The waitress came with their drinks.

After they ate, they got down to business. Laura got out a piece of paper that had three columns with each of their names on top. Under each name were four categories:

Hair:
Nails:
Dress:
Shoes:

Chloe, looking across the table, saw that Laura's and Jace's columns were filled in. Laura had long elaborate descriptions next to hers.

"All right, Chloe," said Laura, "let's figure you out. What are you doing with your hair?"

"Uhm . . . nothing?" said Chloe, a little defensively.

"Are you sure?" said Laura. "Other people will be getting theirs done."

Chloe wasn't totally sure. But she was pretty sure.

"How about your nails?" said Laura. "If we make you an appointment will you come with us to the manicure place?"

Chloe nodded that she would. Laura wrote it down.

"And what's your dress situation?"

"Brian's helping me."

"Okay, but like what sort of thing are we talking about?"

"I don't know exactly," said Chloe.

"But, like, black, white, yellow, green?"

"How would I know? We haven't gone shopping yet."

"Don't worry," said Jace. "Brian will hook her up."

"I hope so," said Laura. "What about shoes? Can I put you down for strappy sandals?"

Chloe saw that Laura and Jace both had "strappy sandals" in their shoe category. "If you want," said Chloe.

"Do you *have* strappy sandals?"

"No."

"Do you want to borrow some?"

"Do I have to?"

"No, Chloe. But strappy sandals are kind of the obvious thing."

"What about . . . PRO-Keds?" said Chloe.

"Chloe, it's a formal event. You need real shoes. High heels, sandals, that sort of thing."

"But my feet are ugly."

"Your feet are fine."

"Actually," said Jace. "Her feet are a little weird."

"I'm already getting a dress," said Chloe, "can't I wear something normal on my feet?"

"Dress shoes are normal," stated Laura. "When you're wearing a dress."

"Don't worry," Jace repeated. "Brian will hook her up."

Fortunately for Chloe, Laura wanted to move on. She wrote down "To Be Determined" next to "Shoes" in Chloe's column.

Next, Laura produced a new piece of paper with a complicated chart drawn on it. It included each person going to the prom, who their date was, who their friends were, who their date's friends were, and who needed to hang out with whom.

"Wow," said Jace, trying to follow all the arrows and circles. "This is like math."

"This is to help us prioritize our social obligations," said Laura. "First, in the center, is us—"

Chloe raised her hand.

"Chloe, you don't have to raise your hand," said Laura.

"I have a question, though."

"What is it?"

"What does Zach look like?"

"I told you," said Laura. "I don't know."

"What do you *think* he looks like?" asked Chloe.

"How would I know? He sounded very nice. He reads a lot. He likes the color yellow."

"He does?" said Chloe. "You asked him that?"

"Yes." She got out the paper that had Zach's answers on it.

"Yellow?" said Jace. "That's a weird color for a boy to like."

"What did Abby say?" said Chloe. "About his looks?"

"Abby said he's tall. And cute. He'll be fine. Stop worrying."

"She does have a right to know," said Jace.

"He's in the same situation," explained Laura. "He doesn't know what Chloe looks like."

"Can we spy on him and check him out?" said Chloe.

"Yeah!" said Jace. "Let's spy on him!"

"I thought you didn't want to meet him?" said Laura.

"When did I say that?" said Chloe.

"Before. You said you didn't care who it was."

"Well," said Chloe. "Now that it's an actual person, now I care."

"We can't find him this weekend, anyway," said Laura. "He's going with his dad to pick up some farm equipment."

Chloe and Jace both frowned.

"And we have other things to worry about. We have preparations to make."

"Does he want to meet me?" said Chloe.

Laura sighed. "I'm sure he does. But he understands the situation, and he's fine with meeting you there. That's what you do."

"I wonder what kind of girls he likes," said Chloe, dipping her finger into her water glass.

"As a matter of fact, I asked him that," said Laura looking at the paper. "He likes girls who are easy to talk to and fun to hang out with."

"Like *that* tells us anything," said Jace.

"Everyone likes someone who's easy to talk to," said Chloe. "He's not very original, is he?"

"I told him you were highly articulate and that your dad's a college professor," said Laura. "And also that you're intelligent and sensitive and artistic."

"Lau-*ra*," protested Chloe. "That makes me sound *horrible*."

"What would you want me to say?" said Laura.

"Did you tell him what I looked like?"

"No. But he was very excited. He thinks you sound great. So don't worry. Now let's get back to this."

The three of them went back to the social chart.

"What if Paul wants to hang out with the other tennis players?" said Jace.

"Do you think he will?" asked Laura.

Jace hesitated. She hadn't mentioned Paul's confession to her friends. "He might. He doesn't like big social things. He'll probably want to stay near people he knows."

"Why is he so shy?" asked Chloe. "If he's such a great tennis player?"

"He's kind of not what you expect," said Jace. "Once you get to know him."

"Well, just in case . . ." Laura drew a new area, which she labeled: "Tennis People."

"Good," said Jace.

"Now we have to figure out how to connect all these people and what parties we might want to go to and whose limo we'll go in and what kind of pre-prom stuff will be going on. Also we have to do pictures. And get dinner reservations. I was thinking Alberto's Italian. We can do pictures in a couple places. Maybe we could do a round at my house and then go to Daniel's after."

"I want to see Zach," said Chloe, who was bored. "Can't I even talk to him?"

"Chloe, I would advise you not to do anything. Go along with the process. This is prom. Lots of people get fixed up."

"But what if I hate him?" said Chloe, sticking her finger in her water glass again. "Or what if he's gorgeous and I fall hopelessly in love with him and he thinks I'm a freak? That's probably what'll happen. Oh my God. This is going to be a disaster."

"If you don't act like a freak, he won't think you are one," said Laura. "Take your finger out of your water."

23

The next day, Laura skipped lunch and drove as fast as she dared to Woodridge Mall. She hurried to Springtime in Paris. A different saleswoman brought out Laura's dress. Laura studied the fabric and checked the seams. She was still unsure if it was worth the $349, or the inevitable fight she would have with her mother. She took it to the mirror and held it in front of herself. The lovely olive-cream color still set off Laura's eyes the way it first had. The exposure of her shoulders and neck would still emphasize her soft, milk-white skin, though Laura could see that her face was showing the strain of the last week. She would have to increase her sleeping time. They said that in all the prom books—to make sure you were rested and fresh.

The saleswoman asked Laura when her prom was. Laura told her nine days. The older woman raised her eyebrows at that. Laura needed to make her decision today, to have all the adjustments and alterations done in time, and even that was getting risky.

Laura explained she had to get back to school. She didn't want to rush things and would come back later. But then, before she could reconsider, Laura pulled out her debit card. "But I'll pay for it now."

The saleswoman, a little surprised, took the card to the counter. Two minutes later it was done. Laura walked out of Springtime in Paris the owner of a 349-dollar prom dress.

On her way out, Laura passed Victoria's Secret. As usual, Laura stared inside at the beautiful lingerie. The magazines always encouraged girls to spice things up for their boyfriends with such things. She had never done it. The truth was Laura was afraid of Victoria's Secret. She'd only been there with other people, and then she'd been too embarrassed to seriously look at anything. Plus, she knew her mother would never approve. If she did buy something there, she would have to hide it and wash it in secret—it was too much bother. On the other hand, she was almost a senior now. At some point, her underwear would surely become her own business, wouldn't it?

Having just blown $349 on a dress, Laura felt empowered. She turned on her heel and marched into Victoria's Secret. Underwear for the prom was a valid expense, and she didn't care what her mother thought. The first thing she saw she liked. A silk, pink panties-and-camisole set with lace trim. She found her size and took it to the dressing room. On the way she saw a black lace bra in her size. She grabbed that, too.

In the dressing room, the camisole fit perfectly. It brought out all the right curves. She slipped the lace panties on, over her own, to get the full effect. She was transformed. The look was not "rich girl slut" like she had expected, but something elegant and classical. She turned from side to side—the feeling of it, *silk*, was pure luxury. She took off the camisole and put on the black lace bra. It was the same: simple, dignified, far more comfortable than she could have imagined. She had not intended to actually buy any of this—she couldn't wear the bra with her prom dress—but now she had another idea: She would buy it and wear it this Friday on her movie date with Mike. The timing was perfect. It would be a little preview. It would get his attention, get him refocused on her. Think how surprised he would be, and how excited. He had complained occasionally about her lack of sexy clothes. He'd get an eyeful on Friday.

24

On Thursday, Chloe had a long, serious conversation with Zach Skinner. She explained to him why, as an artist and a poet, she could not subject herself to the intellectual bondage of a sexual/romantic relationship. She needed to remain free in her heart, in her imagination; she needed her soul to remain untouched, unbounded. Without the pressure of loneliness and alienation, what would drive her creativity?

Of course, Zach wasn't actually *present* for this little

speech—it was more of a practice conversation. And of course it was taking place in the world history section of the Barnes & Noble, with Chloe lying on the floor and talking to her notebook.

"Uh, hello? Chloe?"

Chloe rolled onto her side and looked up. It was Rebecca and Shawnie. "Hey," she said.

"Are you talking to yourself again?"

Chloe rolled back onto her stomach. "I can talk to myself if I want. There's no law against it."

"Yeah, if you want everyone to think you're insane," said Shawnie.

"I don't care what people think," said Chloe.

"Rebecca told me about your adventures at the Lincoln party."

Chloe shrugged. "I hate Lincoln people."

"We could go find those girls," said Shawnie. "And kick their asses."

"Violence doesn't solve problems," Rebecca said, dropping onto the floor next to Chloe.

"Like hell it doesn't," said Shawnie. "Those Lincoln bitches need an ass-kicking." She took her own place on the floor so that all three girls lay together, in a kind of triangle. "That's what you get for going to a Lincoln party, anyway," she said, settling herself. "Those people are the biggest snobs."

"I've put that behind me, anyway," announced Chloe. "I have a date."

"For the prom? You do?" Rebecca gasped. "Oh my God, who is it?"

"His name is Zach," said Chloe, with drama in her voice. "Zach Skinner."

"Whoaaa," said Rebecca.

"He'll probably demand sex and then leave you on some dark road somewhere," said Shawnie.

"No, he won't," Rebecca said to Shawnie. "Why can't you be a little positive?"

"He goes to Glencoe," said Chloe.

"Oh great," said Shawnie. "He'll drive you there on his *tractor* and leave you."

"As a matter of fact, his parents are starting an organic farm," said Chloe.

"So what's he look like?" said Rebecca.

"I don't know yet."

"Are you going to find out? Before you go?"

"Possibly not," said Chloe.

"This is like a blind date!" said Rebecca.

"He's friends with that girl Abby who works at Girl Talk," said Chloe.

"The punk girl," said Rebecca. "That should be good. She's sort of cool."

"She's not *cool*," said Shawnie. "She's a *poser*. Any real punk would eat her for breakfast."

"I thought you said there were no real punks anymore," Rebecca said to Shawnie.

"Zach," said Chloe, to herself. "Zachary. Zach *Skinner.*"

"Are you going to sleep with him?" said Shawnie.

"I might," said Chloe. "I have to see him first."

"Really?" said Rebecca. "You would sleep with him? On your first date?"

"She won't sleep with him," scoffed Shawnie. "She's just saying that."

At that moment, some poor soul, an adult, wandered into the Barnes & Noble world history section. He appeared to be, of all things, looking for a book on world history.

Shawnie took offense. "Hel-*lo*?" she snarled at the man. "Can I help you?"

The man looked at her hair, at her lip ring. "No, I guess not," he said meekly. He retreated to the next aisle.

"I bet he'll be cute," said Rebecca. "If he's friends with Abby."

Chloe said nothing.

"Have you got a prom dress yet?" said Shawnie.

"Brian's taking me," said Chloe. "He knows a vintage place."

"Don't spend more than two hundred dollars," said Rebecca. "That's what I heard."

"A prom dress," snorted Shawnie. "I can't think of a bigger waste of money. Think how much you could buy at Salvation Army with two hundred dollars."

"I know," said Chloe. She cocked her head to one side as she drew. "Hello, *Mister* Skinner," she whispered to herself.

"Could you please stop doing that?" asked Shawnie.

"Go somewhere else if you don't like it," said Chloe, who was impervious to criticism, now that she had a date, now that she was going to the prom with a boy named Zach.

25

On Friday the prom buzz began in earnest. The big day was now one week away. The entire school began to vibrate with prom talk and activity. Everywhere on campus, packs of girls gathered, whispered, giggled, and conspired. Innocent as most of it was, Chloe felt a wave of paranoia surge through her. It was the popular people who were the most excited. Or so it seemed. Popular people couldn't really hurt you if you stayed away from them. But she would be there, at the prom, on their turf. Would they laugh at her or torment her in some way? This whole thing could be a replay of the Lincoln party, a total disaster, or worse, a brutal ambush.

That afternoon Chloe did what she always did when she felt a dark mood coming on. She skipped class, hid in the library, and wrote. She started a poem called "Evil Girls," but it was silly and obvious and she abandoned it after a few lines.

Then she thought about Zach. She had tried to stop obsessing over him, and managed it most of the morning.

Now it was hopeless. He was all she wanted to think about. She got out her notebook and tried another poem:

boy, date,
zach who
likes yellow,
zach who is
tall, will like me
or not (nothing to
be done)
we'll take
pictures, dance, run through
the streets,
maybe one moment of
"yes, the stars are lovely,
and the trees are like kings"
and then:
okay,
thanks,
see ya,
good night
   (they say
   i'll remember you forever)

Chloe read it again. She rewrote it on the next page and found she didn't want to change a word. It still needed a title, though, which presented itself easily enough. Chloe went back to the top of the page and wrote, "prom anonymous."

26

That afternoon, Springtime in Paris was so filled with anxious prom-goers, Laura had to wait twenty minutes before she could get someone to help her. Then it took forever for the assistant manager to find her dress. Where was the nice saleswoman? But once she held the soft fabric in her hands, Laura felt warm and tingly all over.

At home, Laura ran upstairs and put on her prom dress. It was stunning. She literally gasped at the sight of it. But something was wrong in the back; something was catching. She could see the tiny crinkle in the fabric when she stood in front of the double mirrors. "Nana!" she called out.

Nana, of course, could fix it. Nana could fix anything. But Nana was also smart. "So this is the dress you found for a hundred and eighty-nine dollars?" she asked while the two of them worked out the imperfection.

"Uh . . . yeah," lied Laura.

"It's awfully nice material," said Nana, watching Laura's face.

"Yeah, the lady said it's usually a lot more. It was on sale."

"A prom dress? On sale? In May? You'll need a better story than that for your mother."

Her mother had just come home from the grocery store. Laura could hear her downstairs and looked fearfully at the door when her mother's heavy footsteps came up the stairs.

"And this label, from New York—it looks awfully fancy. You might want to get rid of that."

Laura snatched a pair of sewing scissors and delicately began poking at the tiny threads around the label.

Her mother entered the room. "Oh look, you got your dress."

"Yeah," said Laura too quickly. "Nana's helping me with it."

Her mother leaned over Laura's shoulder to look. "It's lovely," said her mother. She touched it. "Feel how soft it is. What's it made of?"

Laura moved the scissors discreetly away from the label.

"And it's from New York," continued her mother. "And look how it's sewn. This was the one that cost one hundred and eighty-nine dollars?"

Laura nodded numbly.

"Are you sure?" asked her mother, studying her daughter's face.

Laura tried to nod. But she couldn't.

"Laura, how much did this dress cost?" said her mother, changing tone.

"It turned out to be a little more than one eighty-nine," said Laura.

"How much more?"

"It was . . . I'm not sure, I can't remember."

"Laura Truman," said her mother gravely. "I told you. You are not to waste money on something you'll only wear once."

"But, Mom," stammered Laura. "I can wear it next year, too. And I can lend it to people."

"Who are you going to lend it to?"

"Chloe?"

"Chloe's going *with you*," reminded her mother.

"Maybe this is something Laura has to learn for herself," said Nana, quietly.

"Yeah," said Laura. "And I got some underwear, too. I had to, Mom. All the girls do."

"Since when do you do what all the girls do?"

"I have to do *some* of the things they do; I have a boyfriend!"

Her mother sighed. "I'm going to tell your father about this. And I want to know how much that dress cost."

"It cost a lot and it's my money and I'm not taking it back!" declared Laura.

"Laura, we've talked about this already and it's not open for discussion. You are not allowed to buy outrageously expensive clothes for an event that happens one time in your entire life."

"But that's the thing, it only happens one time in your life!"

"You've already been to a prom. And what did you wear? Do you even remember?"

In fact, Laura remembered it very well. It was an unspectacular, sensibly priced prom dress. Mike had liked it because it came off so easily. Laura remembered seeing it crumpled on the floor beside his bed. Her mother had helped her pick it. It was the last thing on her body before she lost her virginity.

"Mom, I'm seventeen now," said Laura, a slight warble in her voice. "You can't make all my decisions for me."

"We'll see what your father says," said Mrs. Truman. She went downstairs.

Nana continued her work. She spent the next two hours applying tiny but essential adjustments the people at the mall were too hurried or inexperienced to make. When she was done, the dress was so beautiful tears came into Laura's eyes.

Fortunately Nana was there to comfort her.

27

What Laura's father said, when presented with the prom-dress controversy, was: "I need a drink. I had a terrible day at work." Then, as three generations of Truman women stood before him, still wanting a verdict, he loosened his tie and said, "She's seventeen, it's her money, let her do what she wants."

Laura, afraid to hang around lest this victory somehow be taken from her, quietly turned and left the room. Then she sprinted up the stairs to prepare for her movie date with Mike.

Fortunately, no new complications arose, and at seven o'clock Mike arrived to take her to the Woodridge Cineplex. Laura wore her black lace bra. It had a sleek, sexy look, but only if you could see it, and so Laura slyly unfastened her top two buttons as she got into Mike's Jeep Cherokee. As they drove, she continuously arranged her shirt and posture in hope of drawing Mike's attention to the way the bra shaped and lifted her breasts.

He didn't notice. "A bunch of people are going to Daniel's later—wanna go?" he said.

"Who'll be there?"

"Everybody. Daniel, Marianne, all those guys."

"I sort of like how we walk around the mall afterward."

"We can do that anytime. It's a *mall*; it's not like it's going anywhere."

Laura looked out her window. "Everyone likes Marianne and Christine now," she said. "It's weird how popular they've gotten."

"Why's it so weird?" said Mike, displeased. "They're fun girls. They like to party."

"They're so showy about it. They think they're the Hilton sisters."

"So? At least they're not uptight about everything."

Laura watched a Coors Light billboard go by. It featured two blonde twins, their enormous identical breasts bulging out of their bikinis. "Do you think I'm uptight?"

"No. I don't mean you. Just, you know, the people who criticize them. They're seniors. It's different when you're a senior. People don't understand that."

In the movie theater, Laura and Mike waited for the previews to start. Mike still hadn't noticed her bra. Laura tried arranging her shirt again. She snuck a peek down at herself. "Have you noticed anything different?" she asked him.

"About what?"

"About how I look."

"I dunno," Mike glanced at her. "Is that a new shirt?"

"No silly. Underneath. I went to Victoria's Secret."

"You did?" said Mike, with genuine interest. "What did you get?"

"This bra."

"Ahhh," said Mike, staring at her chest and nodding. "I thought there was something."

"Doesn't it look good?"

"Yeah, it looks awesome."

"And I got some other stuff, too. For the prom."

"Sweet," said Mike, nodding his approval.

But when the lights finally dimmed, Laura was sorry she had mentioned the bra. She should have waited and let him find out for himself. That would be the *cool* way to do it. That's what Marianne or Christine would have done.

28

"Welcome to the Oregon High School Tennis Championships," said a canvas sign that also had Nike swooshes and some local beverage companies on it. Jace and Betsy Julevitz drove past it, into the Tualatin Hills Tennis Center. They had come to see Paul Stoyanovich, who had surprised local tennis watchers by working his way out of the pack and into the semifinals.

Betsy and Jace parked and claimed a spot on the grass slope above the court. Brandon Pratt, of the Pratt Furniture family, was ranked twelfth in the state but would have been much higher had he not been disqualified from two of his matches for, among other things, spitting at his opponents. He was, according to an article in the *Oregonian* that day, the John McEnroe of Oregon tennis. He was a very brash and confident young man.

The match had barely begun when Brandon started shouting at Paul. "That wasn't out!" he screamed. "You're not going to cheat me! Don't think you're going to cheat me!" This first outburst instantly attracted a crowd. Jace and Betsy were suddenly joined by spectators from the other matches. Word quickly spread that there was a "wild one" on court six.

Paul managed to win the first set, despite Brandon Pratt's antics, which included hitting balls at Paul when he knelt down to retie his tennis shoe. Coach Hawkins summoned a tournament official to supervise the match. Jace watched Paul carefully to see how the disruptions affected him. He seemed all right. So far.

The second set stayed close. Pratt settled down and only threw his racquet a couple times. Pratt eventually won it in a tiebreaker. That left the match tied at one set apiece.

It was great tennis, but for Jace it was hard to watch. During the break she and Betsy retreated to the concession stand to get a Coke. They sat for a moment on a picnic bench.

"Have you ever known anyone with mental illness?" Jace asked.

"You mean, besides my whole family?" joked Betsy. She drank her Coke. "Why? Do you know someone?"

"Kinda," said Jace. "A friend of . . . someone my brother knows. I guess he was in a mental hospital. I don't know how you're supposed to act around people like that."

"Don't make any fast movements," joked Betsy.

"No, seriously."

"Actually, my mom knew someone who was schizophrenic. She thought space aliens were talking to her."

"Yeah?" said Jace. "Did she get better?"

"I don't think you get better from stuff like that."

"Really? Don't they have drugs?"

"They can drug you up," said Betsy. "But once you start hanging with the space aliens . . ."

Jace frowned and stirred her Coke.

"Jace, I'm kidding. What do you care? Do you have to hang out with the guy?"

"No. But still. I mean, he's super nice and everything."

"That's one thing I've always noticed," said Betsy. "How nice crazy people are. Like the mentally retarded guys at the supermarket? Do you ever notice how happy they are? Always smiling. Not worried about grades, or college, or any of that crap. They're probably happier than we are."

Jace thought about this. It wasn't making her feel better. "We should probably get back."

When they returned, the final set was under way. Everyone involved in the tennis tournament was now crowded onto the grass slopes around the court. Both players held serve and the game score reached 4–4. Paul served to take the lead. At 40–30, he hit a powerful first serve, got to the net, and hit a sharp volley to win the game. Brandon responded by throwing his tennis racquet at Paul. Paul ducked and the racquet bounced across the court and into the fence. The crowd gasped.

Brandon was now swearing violently after every point. The tournament official told Brandon to "refrain from foul language" or he would forfeit the match.

Brandon did not "refrain," and since there were now several hundred people watching, nobody wanted the match to end in a forfeit. The brash young freshman versus the silent Californian; it was too good not to let them fight it out. The match continued.

Now ahead 6–5, Paul reached match point twice but Brandon fought him off. It was then that Jace noticed a television crew coming down the grass hill. A female sportscaster she had seen on TV was carrying a KGW microphone. She looked around more and saw that the entire top of the hill was packed with spectators—the hill *and* the parking lot. There were more people than she had ever seen at a high school tennis match.

"Hey Betsy," she whispered to her friend. "Would you do me a favor?"

"What?"

"Would you get your car, and pull it up here?"

"Why?"

"When this is over, Paul's going to want to leave. Like fast."

29

But Brandon Pratt was not going down easily. On the brink of defeat, he won three points in a row to tie the set at 6-6. That forced a tiebreaker. The crowd loved it. People yelled things down at the players. Brandon seemed to feed on the attention and the energy of the crowd. Paul seemed perplexed by it. It seemed to pain him. But he fought on.

Brandon double-faulted to start the tiebreaker. The crowd groaned, and Brandon slammed his racquet down. The official did not say a word. Paul served, Brandon served, long spectacular rallies were oohed and aahed by the crowd. A woman behind Jace said that if Brandon won this match today, he would dominate Oregon tennis for the next four years.

"That other boy is from California, anyway," said another woman. "He's not even from here."

"He doesn't want it as bad as the Pratt kid," said a man. "He's not as aggressive."

This infuriated Jace, but she said nothing. At that moment, though, something happened to Paul. It was as if he heard the people, too. He had started his serve and suddenly stopped and stepped back from the service line. He looked at the ball, tossed it once in the air, watched it fall. It was an odd thing to do at such a critical moment. The crowd did not like it.

Paul went back to the service line. There was a new expression on his face, a calm resolve. Brandon seemed to feel this shift in his opponent's demeanor. He dug in and prepared himself. No matter what Paul did, he was determined to win the next point.

He did not win the next point. After that, he did not win *any* points. Paul's serve seemed to explode with power. Brandon couldn't handle it. On the next serve Paul aced him. Brandon was speechless. The crowd was suddenly silenced as well. Jace's whole body shivered with excitement. A new Paul was on the court. Brandon served two of his best serves and Paul pounded them both back for winners. Jace could hardly believe her eyes. She and Betsy clutched each other with excitement.

The crowd was less happy. What was happening to their Brandon?

Paul served for match point. The ball hit Brandon's racquet so hard it flew over the fence behind him. The crowd was stunned. "What the *f*—!?" screamed Brandon, a single voice in the silence.

Paul walked to the net to shake hands. Brandon stayed where he was, refusing him. So Paul walked to the bench, gathered his stuff, and strode off the court. The TV crew ran to intercept him.

"Get your car," Jace told Betsy. "Hurry!"

Betsy ran to her car, which was parked against the curb.

Paul walked up the grass hill. The TV lady chased him. A crowd of other people followed him, gawked at him, congratulated him. A small boy in tennis sweats asked for his autograph.

"Go back to California!" called someone from the crowd.

"Booo!" yelled another person from the same direction.

"Paul," said Jace, not yelling but putting the necessary volume into her voice.

Paul heard Jace's voice and found her in the crowd. Jace nodded her head toward Betsy's car. Paul saw it and walked to it. Jace did the same. As if they had practiced it, Paul and Jace both jumped into the backseat of Betsy's Saab. Betsy, who had not quite understood what Jace was planning, understood now. As soon as the doors closed, she pulled forward. She steered quickly through the gathering crowd.

They drove through the parking lot, still being pursued by the TV crew. Paul and Jace both glanced back as they pulled out of the parking lot. The female sportscaster stood in the road, her hands on her hips.

Paul sat back in the seat. There was nothing victorious in his face. No joy, no happiness. He turned to Jace and only then did he smile. "Thanks for getting me out of there," he said.

"No problem," said Jace. "Thanks for beating that jerk."

"You were awesome!" said Betsy from the front seat. "That was the best tennis match I've ever seen!"

"They really loved that guy," said Paul.

"But they loved you, too," said Jace.

"No they didn't," said Paul. "But that's okay. It's over. That's all I care about."

"You're going to the finals," said Betsy. "You're going to win state! You'll be the first ever from Evergreen!"

Paul said nothing.

30

Chloe was thinking about sex. She was sitting by herself in the TV room, sprawled on the couch, her feet up, a pencil in her mouth. Chloe thought about Laura and Mike. She thought about other couples at her school who had done it. She thought about Abby Maxwell who supposedly did it with some punk guy at the mall and didn't even care if he didn't call her. Sex was so messy. It was so weird. It was like doing the weirdest, grossest, most personal thing and having some stranger there watching you.

Chloe stared at the blank TV screen. She chewed on her pencil.

And the people you did it with; you were never free of them. Once you had sex with a person, they were part of you, they never left you. They were in your psyche for the rest of your life. And whatever made you do it in the first place, if you were drunk, or mad at your parents, or you just thought the guy was hot—that one little quirk in your personality had now affected your entire life. And it added up. You started with a blank slate and slowly over the course of your life the "people you slept with" began to form a line in your soul. Maybe there'd be lots of them—a dozen, a hundred even, or maybe only two or three—but there they were, like a criminal lineup. They were your doing. You picked them. You let them be part of you. And you could never send them away or get rid of them. You could never start over. You could never go back.

Dylan entered the room. He picked up the remote, threw himself on the couch, and turned on the TV. He selected VH1. *I Love the 80s* was on.

"Do you mind? I'm reading?" said Chloe, who had *Heart of Darkness* on her lap.

"Read in your bedroom," said Dylan.

"At least turn it to something else," said Chloe. "I hate this show."

"I like it," said Dylan.

"You weren't even born in the eighties," said Chloe.

"So?"

They showed a clip from *The Breakfast Club*. "You don't remember *The Breakfast Club*," said Chloe.

"Neither do you."

They both watched while *The Breakfast Club* was analyzed by several famous TV actors.

"So have you got your prom dress?" teased Dylan.

"No," said Chloe.

"No? You better get it. You're supposed to have it by now. There won't be any left."

"How do you know so much about it?"

"Everyone knows about the prom."

Chloe frowned at her brother. Unfortunately it was

true; everyone seemed to know more about these things than she did. Even her thirteen-year-old brother. It was another reason Chloe felt no guilt in hating him.

Finally he got bored and left the room. Chloe sat for a while by herself, watching the TV. Then she turned to a secret page in her notebook. It was a poem she had started in study hall:

BEFORE/AFTER

Already, I am
in your spell, your
tall dark Zach-ness, a
dreamscape
where you live, where I
go and meet you.
It is quiet there, the
slow tragedy, unfolding.
It is the best part of love,
the silent impossibility.

"Now what are you doing?" said Dylan, who had returned. "Writing a *po-em*?"

Chloe glared at him. "I'm studying."

"No you're not, you're writing a poem. I can tell because your forehead gets a big crease right here." He pointed to the space between his eyebrows.

"How would you like to die?"

"What did I do? I'm just asking." He plopped on his side of the couch. "So who's your prom date?"

"None of your business."

"I can find out, if you don't tell me," he said. He began kicking his legs against the base of the couch. "It's probably some loser, anyway."

"Mom!" shouted Chloe.

"What, honey?" called her mom from the kitchen.

"Dylan is making fun of me about the prom!"

"Dylan, what did we talk about?" said their mother, from the kitchen. "We support each other in this house."

"Why do I have to be supportive, I'm not the parents," Dylan yelled toward the kitchen.

"He said my date is a loser," yelled Chloe. "And he won't stop watching *I Love the 80s*."

"Dylan, honey, you weren't even born then," said their mother.

"Why does everyone keep saying that!" whined Dylan.

Mrs. Thomas, who was going upstairs anyway, came to see for herself what was happening on *I Love the 80s*. The commentators were discussing *Valley Girl* speak and how everyone in the eighties said "totally" and "like."

"I, like, totally remember that," joked Mrs. Thomas.

"Gawd, Mom!" moaned Dylan.

Chloe, disgusted beyond words, retreated upstairs to her room. She had some obsessing to do, anyway. She turned off all the lights and lay on her bed. For a long time she did nothing but stare out the window at the streetlight in front of the neighbors' house. Then, slowly, Zach came to her. She imagined him in a tux, or a suit coat. He would crawl onto the bed beside her, his hands touching her, caressing her, exploring her chest, her legs, tentatively at first, but gradually with more purpose.

"Zach?" she'd ask him.

"Yes?" he'd answer.

"Should we be doing this?"

"I'd stop myself if I could. But I can't."

It would go on like that. His breath on her face, the first kiss, his body on hers, grinding against her. She would touch his hair, his neck, she would slide her hands inside *his* shirt. . . .

There was a loud *clunk* and Chloe's whole room rumbled. Mr. Thomas had turned on the automatic garage door opener. It was so typical. Could he just for once not be so *suburban*? Chloe hated her family. She sat up and went to her desk. She turned on her desk lamp and pointed it into the desktop, so it lit only the surface of her desk and nothing else. In the darkness, she wrote:

Zach, quiet
conqueror of my
heart, motionless, speechless,
without a word.
I wait for you like a
flower in a field,
bright and sweet in my flower
uniform
surrounded by my

innocent flower friends
I want to be mowed down
by you, taken,
obliterated.

31

At Staples on Monday, Laura bent over a prom quiz Abby had found in *CosmoGirl*. Laura, who normally did not have time for magazine quizzes, found herself deep in thought:

Which best describes your prom date:
—friend, nothing more
—friend, hoping for more
—new boyfriend (under three weeks)
—serious boyfriend (over three weeks)
—blind date

Laura checked serious boyfriend with a certain satisfaction, but found it odd that the amount of time used to separate *new* from *serious* was a mere three weeks. Shouldn't it be more like six weeks? Or really three months? How serious can you get in three weeks? What they really should have asked was if you'd had sex with him yet.

What are your expectations for prom?
—fun with friends, nothing more
—some romance/some fun
—a time to share with that special
  someone

Laura thought about her first prom. That had definitely fallen into the "a time to share with that special someone" category. And it had been great. But the fact was, unless you were at the beginning of a relationship, it was kind of a waste to spend all your time at prom with your boyfriend. You could spend time with him anytime. She checked "some romance/some fun."

"Hey!" said a male voice. It was Ryan. He was standing in front of her.

"Oh!" she said, momentarily losing her ability to speak.

"What are you doing?" he said. "Homework?"

"No . . . just some . . . quiz," stammered Laura, sliding it under the counter.

"You looked so serious."

"No . . . I was just . . ." She managed a less serious smile. "What are you doing?"

"Nothing," said Ryan. "I was gonna get a mocha over at Starbucks. You want anything?"

"Oh . . . no, but thanks."

"Do you want to come?"

"Come with you?"

"Yeah, walk over there with me."

"Oh," said Laura. "Uh . . . no . . . I can't." But she did have a break coming up. She could take it now if she wanted. "I mean . . . maybe I . . . I guess I could."

She took off her Staples apron and stuffed it under the counter. There were no customers; nothing was going on. She came around the counter, feeling somehow exposed as she did. Not that Ryan was looking at her, but she suddenly felt acutely aware of her hair, her hips, the way she walked.

They headed down the main concourse. "You're a junior, right?" said Ryan. "Did you guys do Shakespeare this year?"

"Sure," said Laura, but she couldn't remember anything about her classes. Not at that moment.

"I have to write this term paper on *Twelfth Night* before school lets out."

"Oh," said Laura. "That sucks."

"I know. I hate Shakespeare. How does anyone understand it? I know you're supposed to read the Cliffs Notes, but I don't even understand those."

"Shakespeare's impossible," agreed Laura.

"I mean, I like old books sometimes. We read *The War of the Worlds*. That was awesome."

The two walked by Muzik Express. There was a big sign for a music festival concert in the window. "You ever go to concerts?" asked Ryan.

"Sure," said Laura calmly. But in her head confusion

reigned. Why was she with this boy? What were they talking about? What was happening? Her head felt light. Her legs were not walking normally.

At Starbucks she went to the counter where they kept a pitcher of water. She poured herself a plastic cup and drank it.

"You want something?" said Ryan.

She shook her head.

"C'mon, let me get you something," said Ryan. "You didn't charge me for those copies that time."

She let him buy her a decaf latte. They found a table by the entrance. She felt sure a friend of Mike's might appear at any moment. She wasn't doing anything wrong, was she? She was just sitting with a friend.

"I'm in a mocha phase," Ryan confided. "I always used to get lattes."

"I have a boyfriend," said Laura, unable to stop herself.

"You do?" said Ryan. A stricken look crossed his face. He recovered quickly, shifting in his chair and then smiling awkwardly. "I guess that makes sense. You being so cute and all."

Laura nodded bashfully. She couldn't think of what to say next.

Ryan couldn't think of anything to say, either.

"I mean, it's okay," said Laura. "We can still talk and have coffee."

"Sure," said Ryan, staring into his mocha.

"We're going to the prom," said Laura. "My boyfriend

and I. We've been going out a long time. Fourteen months. It's kind of a record. I mean, not for our whole school."

"No, that's cool," managed Ryan. "He's probably an awesome guy."

"He is. He's, like . . . well, he's a senior so he's sort of bored with stuff. We went to the prom last year and we're going again this year and it's sort of like . . . he wants to hang out with his friends and I want to hang out with my friends and it's a little weird."

"Huh," said Ryan. He was losing his courage now. He couldn't look at Laura. He drank his mocha. His face, which had been so open and happy thirty seconds ago, was now visibly pained.

"Oh God," said Laura. "I'm sorry. I shouldn't have said that. I shouldn't have assumed . . ."

"No, no," said Ryan. "That's okay."

"Maybe I should go back—"

"You don't have to," said Ryan.

They both shut up for a moment. Ryan finally managed to smile at her. Laura stirred her latte. People walked by in the mall concourse.

"Really," said Ryan. "It's no biggie."

"I mean, I'm totally glad," said Laura. "That I met you."

"We can just hang."

"Yeah," said Laura. "We totally can."

After they finished their coffees Ryan walked Laura back to Staples. Walking, they seemed to regain their composure. When they passed a shoe display of new Nikes, Ryan stopped to look at them. "These are cool. I wouldn't pay a hundred and twenty bucks, though."

"Oh my God," said Laura. "You should have seen the trouble I got in about my prom dress. It was way more than my parents wanted me to spend. But my grandmother—Nana, I call her—she's so great, she kind of came to my rescue."

"Yeah my parents freak out when I buy stuff. It's like they don't understand you have to look a certain way."

"Oh my God, and my dad, because he grew up in, like, Michigan, he figures . . ."

And so they walked through the mall, talking again, getting comfortable again, feeling bits of sudden happiness and surprise and wonder at the other person. Laura remembered early conversations with Mike that had been like that. She had assumed it was a once-in-a-lifetime thing. But here it was again. That feeling of *beginning*, that feeling of first coming together with someone.

Back at Staples, as she tied her apron back on and watched Ryan disappear down the concourse, she felt overwhelmed by the richness of life, how much there was of it, how it never stopped coming at you. She was not in love with Ryan. She wouldn't let herself be. But wasn't it amazing how there was newness everywhere? The world was infinite, the possibilities endless. Her head reeled with the scope of it.

32

"I feel like it's too late," Chloe told Brian Haggert on Tuesday, as they drove downtown. "Won't the good prom dresses be gone?"

"Not where we're going," he said.

They parked outside a small vintage shop Chloe had never seen before. They went inside. It was not like the Salvation Army she went to. The clothes were fancy and expensive and the owner, a short round woman with a thick gray streak in her hair, smoked constantly. Chloe waved at the air as Brian explained the situation to her. The woman nodded and then led them deeper into the long, narrow store. Clothes were piled to the ceiling, and things slipped off the top shelves as Chloe followed. It was like being in a slowly collapsing mineshaft.

Brian did the talking. They wanted something interesting, cool, different. The round woman listened to him carefully and then began digging through the racks of dresses. Chloe tried several on. They all looked good to Chloe, though as soon as each dress was on her, Brian and the woman began pulling and poking at her. They began to talk as if Chloe weren't there, discussing her bust, her face, her shoulders—but doing so with such attention and seriousness that Chloe was secretly thrilled.

"It's her first prom," said Brian.

"What's the date look like?" said the round woman, biting a lit cigarette as she arranged the hem of the sixth dress Chloe had tried on.

"Don't know," said Brian. "Tall. We don't know anything else."

"A blind prom date," said the woman. "You're a brave girl."

"How about something darker?" said Brian.

"Possibly," said the woman. "And something fuller. What will she do with her hair?"

Brian nudged Chloe.

"Nothing?" said Chloe tentatively.

"Maybe up?" asked the woman. "Or this way?"

The two of them played with Chloe's hair.

"What about this?" said the woman, touching Chloe's red barrette.

"It's her trademark," said Brian.

"Hmmm."

"She's a big fan of Sylvia Plath."

"Yes, I can see that," said the woman.

"Do you have something darker?" asked Brian.

"I do have a wonderful cocktail dress. It's a little more Audrey Hepburn. . . ."

"Audrey Hepburn?" gulped Chloe. Audrey Hepburn was her second favorite historical figure.

"Let's try it."

The Audrey Hepburn dress was brought out. It was the simplest of the dresses. It was black with a black velvet belt. Chloe put it on. At first, as she wiggled into it, it felt too small. Then for a moment, it seemed too big in the shoulders. And then, as Brian gawked, and the round woman stepped back, it fell over her body and seemed to melt into place.

"Oh. My. God," whispered Brian.

"That's the one," said the little round woman, taking a drag from her cigarette and poking Chloe in the breast. "Maybe bring this in a touch."

When Chloe saw herself in the mirror she almost fell over. It was not a different person, as sometimes happened with good clothes. No, it was still Chloe. But it was the best Chloe. The most precise, composed, indomitable Chloe. The Chloe she would have to be, to survive what was coming.

"What about shoes?" said the woman, lighting a cigarette and watching Chloe's bare feet.

"Chloe?" said Brian. "What about shoes?"

Chloe, lost in her own reflection, didn't answer.

"I think we're going to need some," Brian said quietly to the woman. "Can you show me what you've got?"

33

On Wednesday morning, Jace and her brothers ate Cheerios in the Torres kitchen. Her father came downstairs whistling cheerfully, which Jace always found embarrassing. She ate her Cheerios.

Her brother, who was reading the newspaper, nudged Jace. "Do you know this guy?" he said.

Jace looked. Then she grabbed the page. There, staring out from the front of the sports section, was Paul Stoyanovich. It was not a picture of him playing tennis, it was more like a mug shot. It didn't even look like him. She pulled it away from her brother. The large headline ran above the photo: *Prep Tennis Star Overcomes Obstacles*.

"What on earth . . . ?" murmured Jace.

"You know him?" said her brother.

"Yes, I know him. He's my prom date!"

The other brothers looked. Her dad did, too. The whole family gathered around the paper. Her oldest brother, Carlos, read it aloud:

Paul Stoyanovich is not your average tennis star. A surprise entry in the high school tennis finals today, some consider him a legitimate challenger to number one-ranked Chris Norton. But Stoyanovich's journey to such lofty status has been plagued by personal demons, which the young athlete has struggled to overcome.

A native of San Diego until last year, the young phenom was ranked as high as second in California in his first years on the California Junior circuit. Then disaster struck. . . .

"That's your prom date?" said Jace's dad.

Her stunned expression did not change. She sat in her chair. Her brother continued to read:

. . . after a plea bargain lowered his charge to reckless endangerment he was given a suspended sentence and released into the care of Harwick House, a private psychiatric facility where he was treated for severe depression and bipolar disorder.

Miraculously, through the efforts of his doctors and family, he was able to return home and eventually to play tennis again. Currently, the seventeen-year-old junior at Evergreen High School lives with his uncle and aunt and has started a new life. . . .

"How come they don't have any quotes by him?" asked her brother.

"Because they didn't talk to him," declared Jace, slamming her spoon down. "He never would have told anyone this. How dare they write this!" She stood up and ran to the stairs.

"Jace, honey?" called her father. But Jace ran up the steps two at a time.

In her room she called Paul. A grown-up answered.

"Hello, is Paul there?"

"Who is this, please?" said a woman who must have been Paul's aunt. She sounded very suspicious and very angry.

"Jace. Jace Torres. It's okay. I'm a friend."

Paul came to the phone.

"Paul?" said Jace. "You saw the paper?"

"Yeah," he said, quietly. "The phone's been ringing off the hook."

"Oh my God, what are you going to do?"

"There's not much I can do."

"Are you going to school?"

"I kind of have to," he said. "Or I can't play the match."

"That article was so awful. I can't believe they would print that. Is that even legal?"

"My aunt called my dad. She wants to sue them for libel. But my dad said you can't. It's all public record."

"What about school?" asked Jace. "How are you going to face everybody?"

"I don't know. Just go, I guess."

"Come pick me up," said Jace. "We'll go together."

"You don't have to."

"Paul! Are you kidding!? I am totally going to school with you!"

"Are you sure?"

"Yes!"

Fifteen minutes later, Paul and Jace pulled into the parking lot of Evergreen High School. Jace braced herself. If any girls said anything, she would kick their asses. If any boys said anything, she would kick *their* asses. If several boys ganged up on them, she would go home and get her whole family and kick everyone's ass.

Paul was more calm about things. He parked, got his books, locked the doors with the remote. He maintained his usual demeanor, head down slightly, a gracefulness in his body movements that never seemed to leave him. Jace glanced over at him as they walked and noticed that Paul was as good-looking as she had ever seen him. A quiet resolve had settled into his face.

As they crossed the lawn, Betsy Julevitz ran to join them. She walked on the other side of Paul, not saying a word, but obviously aware of what had happened.

The three of them walked into the junior/senior wing. They walked to Paul's locker. No one said a word. No one seemed to even notice him. Then one kid, a boy from the JV tennis team, nodded at Paul. "Hey bro, good luck today," he said.

"Thanks."

Someone else gave Paul a thumbs-up. A girl wished him luck.

This was not the reaction Jace had expected, but she remained protective. She and Betsy stood on either side of him, while he put his books in his locker.

"Dude!" said a big voice. It was Craig Foltz, one of the varsity football players. "What was all that bullshit in the paper this morning?" he said loudly. Several people turned to listen to him.

Paul shrugged.

"Why don't those dickheads mind their own business? That same guy wrote some crap about me last fall. Said I was on steroids. I almost went down there and knocked his friggin' head off."

Paul smiled.

"You go win us a championship today," said Craig. "That'll shut 'em up."

"Yeah, thanks," said Paul.

Jace said nothing during this exchange but suddenly noticed three girls watching Paul. They were checking him out!

Oh great, thought Jace. *Now everyone's going to fall in love with him.*

34

Chloe's first "book" of poetry started this way: First she rewrote the poem "Prom Anonymous" in her biology notebook, which, since she never took notes in biology, was conveniently empty. Then she wrote "Before/After" and "Flower" in her English notebook, underneath two John Donne poems. Then she wrote a poem called "Take It Back, Zach" in the margins of her Culture and Society textbook. Then she wrote two sex poems on an old knitting club flyer she found in her locker. It was at this point that she decided to buy a little notebook and recopy all the Zach poems in one place. She liked the idea of a complete set of poems, all on one subject, all in one place. It would be her own little book, like *Ariel* by Sylvia Plath.

She went to the Turner's Discount Store across from Evergreen and with great care selected a medium-sized Mead notebook (with a yellow cover, naturally).

The recopying she did in Spanish class and the study period after. No sooner had she rewritten the earlier poems, then she wrote two new short poems, one after the other. Later, in biology, she wrote a two-page poem called "Yellow."

And she kept going. By midweek she had twenty-one Zach poems. Not only was this a record for her, it was also an artistic breakthrough. Something was happening in her writing, a new honesty, a new urgency. Previously it took her days to finish one poem. Now, with the looming form of Zach filling her every thought, she could write two or three in an hour—she could write them as fast as she could move her hand. And while there were obvious lapses in the quality, far more important were the occasional bursts that were better than anything she had ever done before. By going fast, by not thinking, by letting the tension of the Zach situation drive her, she found that all sorts of surprising things popped out of her pen.

She didn't tell anyone about the notebook, and on Wednesday afternoon she went to Barnes & Noble like she always did. Rebecca, Shawnie, and Brian were on the floor in the world history section. Rebecca wanted to know what was next in the prom countdown. She had become as absorbed in the prom process as Chloe was, if not more. "Are you going to get your hair done?" she asked.

"No," said Chloe.

"If you guys start talking about stupid prom stuff, I'm leaving," declared Shawnie.

"Are you going to wear your barrette?" asked Rebecca.

"Yes, she is," Brian answered for her. "You guys won't believe how awesome Chloe is going to look."

"I wish I could see it," said Rebecca, wistfully.

"You can't," said Shawnie. "So don't get your panties in a twist."

"I could go watch the pictures and stuff," said Rebecca to Shawnie. Then to Chloe: "Where are you guys taking pictures?"

"Laura's, I think," said Chloe, who hadn't thought about pictures.

"You're really obsessed with prom," Brian said to Rebecca.

"No, I'm not," said Rebecca.

"You can go, you know," Brian told her.

"No I can't."

"Of course you can."

"How?"

"You just go."

"You can't just *go* to the prom," said Rebecca.

"Why not?" said Brian. "It's your school. They can't turn you away."

"Don't you have to register?"

"Trust me," said Brian. "You show up at the Hilton in a prom dress and nobody's going to kick you out."

Rebecca frowned. In a way, she enjoyed feeling bad about not going to the prom. The possibility that she could actually go made her feel uncomfortable.

Brian's cell phone rang. He turned and answered it. Shawnie scribbled on a large piece of drawing paper. Rebecca leaned against the Napoleonic Era and thought about her life. Chloe lay on her stomach and read through her "Prom Anonymous" poems.

Brian put his hand over the phone. "Did you guys hear this thing about Paul Stoyanovich?"

"What about him?" said Chloe.

"Apparently he's insane," said Brian.

"No he's not," said Chloe.

"Oh yes he is. He was in the loony bin. In California. And now he's playing in some championship tennis thing."

"Oh my God, I'm supposed to go to that," said Chloe, rolling over. Jace had left her a message telling her to come. "Anyone wanna watch a tennis match?" she asked her three friends. At first, no one wanted to. Then Rebecca said she would.

"When does it start?" Chloe asked Brian, as she grabbed her stuff.

"Right now," he said. "Apparently half the school is there."

35

Half the school *was* there. Most of them sat on the grass slopes on the south end of the court. Other students—Chris Norton supporters—sat on the opposite end. There were adults, too, tournament officials, parents, tennis fans, people who had read the article and were curious to see the Stoyanovich kid in the flesh.

Jace and Betsy Julevitz sat behind the fence, close to the bench where the players took their breaks. Jace sat with her knees up, her arms crossed over them, so she could bite her nails. Betsy sat with her legs flat against the grass incline. She kicked the toes of her sneakers together, in nervous anticipation. Paul would serve first.

"Jace?" said Chloe, coming down the hill with Rebecca. "Can we watch with you guys?"

"Of course."

The girls scooted over so the four of them formed a line.

The match began. Paul served. Chris Norton hit it back so hard everyone on the hill flinched. Paul lost the point.

"Jace?" whispered Chloe.

"Yeah?" said Jace, watching the next point.

"Did Paul really go to a mental hospital?"

"Yes," said Jace, watching the ball go back and forth.

Wow, thought Chloe, feeling a pang of jealousy— though a "touch of madness" was probably not as much help to a tennis player as it was to a poet.

The match did not go well for Paul. Chris Norton was tall and strong. His serves were overpowering, and when Paul could get a good return, Norton was so quick to the net, Paul would lose the point anyway. The game score went quickly to 2–0, then to 3–1, then 5–1. Paul lost the first set 6–2.

At the break between sets, Paul toweled off and checked his racquet. He walked to the fence and looked into the crowd. He found Jace and waved. She jumped up and ran to the fence.

In front of the hundreds of people gathered, he smiled bashfully at her. "What's up?" he said, as if this was the most ordinary situation in the world.

"Nothing," she said, shyly. "What's up with you?"

"Nothing. I seem to be losing a tennis match."

"Yeah, I noticed."

He grinned at her. "I've been meaning to ask you. Have you got your prom dress yet?"

Jace grinned. "Yes."

"What's it like?"

"It's nice."

"What color is it?"

"Blue," said Jace.

"Navy blue?"

"No lighter," said Jace. "Sort of aqua."

"Oh," said Paul. He looked into her face. "I can't wait to see it," he said.

"I can't wait to show it to you."

The head linesman gestured for the match to resume. Everyone at the Tualatin Hills Tennis Center watched while Paul talked to the cute Hispanic girl, who some of the local sports journalists recognized as "Jace" Torres, star point guard of the Evergreen girls' basketball team.

"Well I'd better get back to this," said Paul.

"Your presence seems to be required," joked Jace.

Paul thought for a moment. He looked around at the court, at the sky, at the crowd. "You know, I'm sure glad we're going to the prom."

"Me, too."

"Mr. Stoyanovich?" said the head linesman. "Can we begin the second set?"

Paul nodded, then he whispered to Jace, "I gotta go."

"I think so," said Jace. "But Paul?"

"Yeah?"

"Maybe hit deep to his backhand?"

"I tried it. It didn't work," said Paul. He winked at her and walked back onto the court.

Jace ran back up the hill. When she looked around, she saw that everyone had been watching her.

"Oh my God!" said Chloe. "You can talk to them? Right in the middle of the game?"

"Shhh!" said Betsy. "It's not a game, it's a match."

"Well *excuuuse* me," said Chloe.

Paul fought valiantly throughout the second set, but was ultimately no match for Chris Norton. He was gracious in defeat, though, shaking Norton's hand and putting his arm around him for the cameras. After that, a huge crowd formed around Norton. Paul was left alone, sitting on the bench with a towel over his head. Jace and Betsy pushed onto the court to get to him. Paul was discouraged but not upset. Jace hugged him and kissed him awkwardly on the cheek. She had never kissed him before.

Then Coach Hawkins appeared, and Doug Rotter and some of the other tennis players. They gathered around, congratulating him. Jace found herself backing away and standing with Chloe and Rebecca. It was Paul's moment. Even though he had lost, everyone was proud of him.

Then Jace's cell phone rang. It was Laura. She wanted everyone to meet later that night to discuss final preparations.

Prom was in two days.

36

"It looks fine," said Mike. "Jeez!"

Laura did not agree. She circled Mike as he stood at the three-paneled mirror at Elite Formal Wear. The rented tuxedo he wore had many problems, the worst being that the pants cuffs were so low they dragged on the ground behind his heel. For some reason they always did that at Elite Formal Wear. So now Laura had to make the guy go back and fix it.

Mike didn't care about the length of his pants. He wanted to leave. "Who cares?" he complained. "It's the cuff, who sees it?"

Laura cared. The man took the pants back into the alterations room. Laura and Mike had to wait.

Mike flopped on the fake leather couch. Laura took her place beside him. "So I saw that thing in the newspaper about Paul Stoyanovich," he said.

Laura nodded that she had seen it, too.

"Jesus," said Mike. "So not only do we have Chloe the freak coming with us, now we got Paul the nut-job."

"Paul's not a nut-job."

"Three months in the psycho hospital? That's a nut-job."

"He's very nice and he's Jace's prom date."

"He better not do anything weird at the prom."

"He won't."

"Here you go," said the man, bringing the pants back out.

"We'll need to try them on again," Laura told the man.

Mike glared at her. "Why do we have to try them on again?" he demanded.

"To make sure they're right," said Laura.

"We know they're right. The guy just fixed them," said Mike. "You fixed them, right?" Mike asked the man.

The man nodded, but Laura was firm. "You have to try them on again. Everything has to be right."

"For chrissakes," said Mike. "Why are you being like this?"

"It'll take three seconds!" insisted Laura.

Mike, furious, nevertheless threw the pants over his arm and went back to the dressing room. Laura waited outside the door. The alterations man stood beside her.

They could both hear Mike cursing as he took off his jeans and put on the tuxedo pants. He came out and stood in the three-paneled mirror.

Laura looked down at his feet. "You have to put your shoes on," she said.

Mike jammed his feet angrily into his shoes. Then, as he and the salesman watched, Laura got down on her hands and knees to inspect the cuff. They were the right length but now she was worried they had done a hasty job, and they might come undone in the middle of the dance.

But the cuffs appeared secure. They were the right length. She was satisfied.

She looked up to tell Mike, but stopped short when she saw his face in the mirror. His expression shocked her. He was shaking his head, a look of utter disgust and exasperation on his face. He hated her. She saw it. He was sick of her, he didn't like her anymore, he didn't want to go to the prom with her. It was all there, in his face, clear as day.

"Mike?" she said, her voice suddenly quiet and weak. *"What?"*

"They're fine. They're good. We can go."

"Thank God!" he said. He stormed back into the dressing room. Laura stood up slowly. Now she looked at herself in the three-paneled mirror. She looked awful: stressed, worn out, pale. She had to turn away.

• • •

At Denny's that night, the three girls and Abby Maxwell sat in a booth. Laura had called the meeting, to go over final preparations. But as she sat there, she appeared dazed, lost. The other girls waited for her to take charge. When she didn't, Chloe asked her where her papers were.

"What papers?"

"You know," said Chloe. "With the circles and the charts and everything."

"Oh," said Laura. "They're in my backpack. Which I forgot."

"So where are we taking pictures?" asked Jace.

"I guess we'll do it at my house. But Mike . . ." Laura caught her breath for a moment. "I think Mike wants to stop by Daniel's, too."

The other girls looked at Laura.

"What restaurant are we going to?" asked Abby.

"I'm not sure," said Laura, without emotion.

"I thought we were going to Alberto's Italian?" said Chloe.

"Are we going in Mike's limo?" asked Jace.

"I don't think so," said Laura.

"Are we getting manicures?" asked Chloe.

"I tried to get us appointments. . . ." said Laura, rubbing her temples.

"You look terrible," Chloe said, suddenly.

"Chloe," said Jace.

"What? She does," said Chloe. "Are you okay?"

All the girls waited for the answer.

"I'm just . . ." Laura felt her voice faltering. "I think Mike is sick of me."

"Really?" asked Chloe.

"Why do you think that?" asked Jace.

"The way he's acting," said Laura. "We were trying on his tux and he got so—"

"Guys hate trying on stuff," said Abby. "That doesn't mean anything."

"He's just stressed," said Jace. "Just like everyone."

"You think that's it?" said Laura.

"Of course," said Jace. "You guys have been together for fourteen months. He *loves* you."

"He totally loves you," said Abby.

Laura found this news cheering. "You think I'm being paranoid?"

"Of course you are," said Jace. "Everything's going to be fine. And if Mike is acting a little weird now, think how great he'll be on prom night. Wasn't he great last year?"

Laura had to admit he was.

It was agreed that Laura and Mike would have a great time. Jace told Laura to relax, that being stressed out was bad for your skin. Abby reminded her that it was springtime and she was young and she should be enjoying herself. No matter what happened.

Only Chloe, who often took the darker view of things, refrained from comment.

37

After Denny's, Laura felt better. Her friends were right; this was a magical time in her life. She was young, pretty, seventeen. She shouldn't waste time worrying about Mike.

On her way home, she stopped at Staples to get the backpack she had forgotten earlier. Most of the shops were closed or closing. Since she'd entered on the south end, she decided to walk on the second level. She wasn't sure why exactly. She just felt like it. She also felt like walking on the right side, the side Happy Pet was on.

Ryan was in the store, vacuuming behind the cash register. Laura was suddenly embarrassed. She hadn't expected him to actually be there. She sped up, hoping he wouldn't see her.

It didn't work. "Hey!" said Ryan, as she passed. "Laura! Hey! What are you doing up here?"

"I was . . ." she said. She had no answer.

"You just get off?"

"No, I was at Denny's. I had to get something." It sounded ridiculous, like an excuse, like she wanted to see him.

"I'm almost done. What are you doing? Can I walk you somewhere?"

"Uh . . ." said Laura.

"Wait here," said Ryan. He wrapped up the vacuum cleaner cord and dragged it into the back. A second later he was back, flushed and happy.

The two of them walked along the second level together. The mall was quiet and empty. Their footsteps echoed in the high ceilings.

"So how's the office supply business?" Ryan asked her.

She shrugged. "Okay, I guess. How's the pet business?"

"Okay," he said, smiling. "Puppies are doing well."

"I guess puppies never go out of style."

"No. Puppies and kittens. You can't really go wrong with that."

They both grinned and walked. When they arrived at Staples, the cleaners were emptying the big trash cans. Laura pulled her backpack out from behind the customer service counter.

"Want to go to Denny's?" said Ryan, as they walked out the southern entrance.

"I was just there," said Laura.

They stepped into the warm spring night. It did something to both of them, woke them up to something.

"Wanna do something else?" asked Ryan. "Go for a walk?"

"I'm kind of . . . I got a lot of stuff to do. . . ." said Laura. Then she thought about what her friends had told her. Prom was supposed to be fun. Springtime was supposed to be fun. Life was supposed to be fun.

"You sure?" said Ryan. "We could check out the Transit Center. They finally finished that waterfall thing."

"Yeah?" she said.

"It's probably stupid or whatever."

Laura looked across the empty mall parking lot. "Well, I guess I could. . . ."

They crossed the parking lot to the Transit Center and the new waterfall sculpture that had just been completed. They stood before it. Water flowed down a series of flat benches into three spotlit pools. It was for people to look at while they waited for the light-rail into the city.

Ryan ventured forward. Laura followed. From behind she watched his skinny arms, his skinny neck, his thick brownish hair. He was not jockish at all, and yet he moved with an easy, boyish confidence. At the end of the walkway, he put his hand under the waterfall so that water sprayed everywhere. "Ahhh!" shrieked Laura, backing away.

Ryan smiled and kept moving. He began to climb the benches, letting the water run over his hands and arms as he did. He did it quickly, smoothly, and in a few seconds he was on top of the falls, perched casually on a cement ledge.

"Come up," he called to her.

She looked at him. "I don't think I can," said Laura.

"Come around the side," said Ryan. "There's steps, and not as much water."

Laura did it. It was an easy climb, but she still managed to splash herself and stick her foot in one of the pools, soaking her tennis shoe. When she got to where Ryan was, she sat beside him and squeezed her wet hands between her legs.

"Nice view of the asphalt," joked Ryan. The two looked out over the empty parking lot. Laura sat close. Their hips touched. She could smell him, little wafts of him mixed in with the smell of the spraying water and the grassy smell of springtime.

"Will we get in trouble, being up here?" asked Laura.

"I dunno. Probably."

They didn't speak for a while. They gazed at the sea of black pavement. Ryan leaned forward slightly. Laura leaned back. This was a good position for her. She could look at him. She could study his back and shoulders. She stuck her nose closer to the back of his shoulder and smelled him, quietly so he wouldn't know.

But then he turned. He turned and looked into her face. He stared at her mouth. It was the same thing Mike did when he was about to kiss her.

Ryan leaned in. He closed his eyes.

"No," said Laura simply, without moving away.

Ryan stopped inches from her face.

"I can't," said Laura.

He studied her expression, to be sure she meant it. She did. His face fell and he turned away.

"I'm sorry," she whispered.

"Don't be."

She looked into her lap. "I just . . . I can't do things like that."

"Yeah, I know. It's my own fault."

"It's not, though," said Laura. "It's just the situation."

Ryan didn't speak. He leaned forward. He stared down into the swirling water.

"Please," said Laura. "Don't feel bad. I'm glad I came. Really. Thank you for bringing me up here."

"Okay," said Ryan, though Laura could tell by the slump in his shoulders it was not okay.

Laura lifted her hand to touch him, to reassure him, to comfort him.

But she found she could not do it, and lowered her hand.

38

On Thursday, the day before the prom, a kicking war broke out at the Thomas residence. "If you're such a sensitive artist, why are you so mean?" said Dylan. He had a point about the meanness. Chloe, from her side of the couch, was kicking him for no apparent reason.

"I never said I was a *sensitive* artist," she said, kicking him one last time for good measure. They were watching *I Love the 70s*. It wasn't as good as the *I Love the 80s*. The videos weren't as good.

"Well, you write all those stupid poems all the time," said Dylan, kicking her. She kicked him back. He kicked her harder.

"Mom!" she cried. "Dylan's kicking me!"

"No, I'm not!" he said.

"You two. Stop it! You're too old to be kicking each other!"

"I know who your prom date is," taunted Dylan.

"No you don't."

"Yes I do."

"Get your foot away from me," said Chloe, kicking him. Her mom came into the room. "Honey, stop kicking your brother."

"He kicked me first!"

"Chloe? You're older. Can you please act like it?" said her mother, shaking her head and disappearing up the stairs.

"You have arrested development," said Dylan.

"You don't even know what that means."

"Yes I do."

"*You* have SDD," she said.

"What's that mean?"

"It means you have spastic dork disease."

"I'm not a spastic dork," said Dylan. "You're the one who wears that stupid barrette. Are you wearing it to *the prom*?" He sang the last two words, for maximum annoyance.

"*Shut. Up,*" said Chloe kicking him once for each word.

Upstairs, the phone rang. Both Chloe and Dylan fell silent for a moment.

"Chloe, phone," called her mother from upstairs.

"It's your *prom date*," sang Dylan.

"No it's not," she hissed at him. To her mom she yelled: "Who is it?"

There was a one-second delay. "It's a boy."

"If it's Brian, tell him I'll call him back."

"It's not," called her mother. "It's someone else. Zach something?"

Chloe's eyes opened wide as saucers. Then she screamed. "Ahhhhhhhh!" she wailed as she jumped off the couch. She began to run. She ran into the kitchen, through the living room, into the front hall, back through the TV room, and up the stairs as her little brother sat watching the terror on his sister's face.

Chloe sprinted up the stairs. "What does he want?" she gasped to her mother.

"How would I know?"

"I'll get it in my room." Chloe ran into her room and shut the door. She locked it. Then she sat on her bed, and took three deep breaths. Then she had a thought. Why was he calling now? Was he canceling?

She lifted the phone. She cradled it in her lap, and

said a silent prayer. Then she lifted it slowly to her ear. "Hello?" she said, gripping it with both hands.

"Hi. Uh . . . is Chloe there?"

"This is Chloe," she answered, her eyes darting madly around the room.

"Oh. Hey. It's Zach."

"Hey, Zach," answered Chloe.

"Uh. Well. My mom said I should, like, call you and ask you what color your dress is."

"Black," blurted Chloe.

"Oh. Okay. Cool. Cause I have to get you a corsage and my mom was saying, you know, that it's polite to call and ask you because of the color or whatever. And she said it was weird that I hadn't talked to you. Do you think it's weird?"

"No. I mean, it's okay. I thought we were going to meet there. I mean, it's fine. Either way. We could talk. Or we could not talk."

"Yeah, that's what I thought. But I figured it wouldn't hurt to talk a little."

"No, it's okay," said Chloe, bouncing slightly on her bed. "We can talk a little."

"So this should be fun, huh?"

"Yeah," said Chloe.

There was a long silence. "Abby said you're into poetry and stuff," said Zach.

"Yeah, sort of. I like poetry."

"Yeah. Poetry's cool."

"What are you into?"

"Just whatever. I just moved so I've been dealing with that. My parents are starting an organic farm."

"Oh."

"Do you think that's weird?" asked Zach. "Starting an organic farm?"

"No. Not at all," said Chloe. "Are your parents hippies?"

"Nah, they look pretty normal. They're just into stuff like that. They're into natural products."

"Oh."

"Yeah," said Zach. "So another thing I wanted to ask you was, how tall are you?"

"Five-seven," said Chloe. "How tall are you?"

"Six-one."

"That's not too bad," said Chloe.

"Yeah we can dance at least. I mean, we can dance with other people, too. You know. If we want to. Or if there's a slow dance . . . or you know . . . something like that. . . ."

"Or for pictures," said Chloe.

"Yeah, pictures."

"One thing about me, Zach?" said Chloe, clutching the phone.

"Yeah?"

"I'm not really the kind of person who goes to proms."

Zach hesitated for a moment. "Yeah? Like, what do you mean?"

"I just don't usually do stuff like that."

"Why are you doing it now?"

"I don't know exactly. I mean, I'm not super ugly or anything. But, like, my real best friends, they're not going."

"Oh."

"Does that make sense?"

"Yeah, I guess."

"Do you think that's weird?"

"No, if that's how you feel."

Chloe waited for him to say more. "Oh God," she breathed. "Now you think I'm a freak."

"No, I don't," he said. "You're just not into it."

"I mean, I'm not *totally* antisocial. I'm just like . . ."

Zach waited for her to finish. She didn't. "It doesn't matter," he said. "My mom's like that. She always has to be different. She made us drink soy milk, you know, before everyone else did."

"Are you like that?"

"Nah. I'll do whatever. I don't care."

Chloe didn't know what to say next.

"Well, I better go," said Zach. "I'll see you tomorrow."

"Okay," said Chloe. "Bye."

✓ DATES
✓ PREP
✓ PROM

39

Prom morning was a typical day in late spring in Portland, Oregon. The air was warm and wet, gray clouds hung low over the treetops, light sprinkles of rain dabbled puddles on quiet streets. While students at Evergreen High School woke up bristling with nervous excitement, most Portlanders did what they always did: Got in their cars. Drove to work. Stopped at Starbucks or Coffee People. No one thought anything of the dark sky, the low clouds, the raindrops on their windshields.

No one except Chloe. To her, the ominous skies were a terrible sign. Disaster awaited her; she could feel it in her bones. She sat in her kitchen, sullenly poking at a bowl of Wheat Chex while her brother chewed his own cereal and read a comic book beside her. Chloe's face was puffy, her eyes swollen; she had obviously not slept well. Among other things, she wished to God she had not told Zach she was the kind of person "who didn't go to proms." *Why did she say that?* He would think she was lame, pathetic, a loser. He would hate her. He would hook up with someone else, right in front of her, right in front of everyone; she would be mocked, laughed at, driven out of the prom, into the street, into the gutter.

Her brother, for once, kept his mouth shut. Chloe's mother, though, could see the strain in her daughter's face. She waited until Dylan left and then gave her daughter a long, deep hug. Chloe, who made it a point never to cry in front of her mother, allowed herself a few nervous tears.

Four blocks away, surrounded by her three brothers, Jace Torres ate instant oatmeal with a nervous twitter in her stomach. The feeling was not unlike the day of a big basketball game. Would things work like they were supposed to? Would Laura's plans come together?

She also had Paul to worry about. In all the excitement she had not thought about what might happen *after* the prom. Laura would probably have after-party plans. Or they'd do something as a group. But what if Paul didn't want to? What if he bailed on her? Or what if the opposite happened and he wanted to go somewhere private and be alone with her?

That would be good, of course; that's what she wanted. . . . Or was it? She realized, as much as she had fought the "just friends" concept, she had used it, too, to shield herself from her own doubts and insecurities. The fact was, Jace had never had a serious boyfriend. She'd never had sex. The most she'd done was some minor groping with a guy at basketball camp who told her she was a lousy kisser, which didn't exactly fill her with confidence. What if Paul wanted to make out? What if he wanted to do *more* than make out? He was from California, after all, where girls were famously promiscuous.

And another thing: Sure, she and Paul were close now, when there were proms and tennis finals and newspaper controversies to bond over. But what about summer, when there was no drama, no natural excuses to hang out? Would their friendship survive? Plus, she had basketball camp coming up, and summer workouts for varsity next year. They'd only hung out during tennis season when he was the star. What would happen during basketball, when the spotlight was on her? Could Paul even handle that?

But she knew the answer. Of course he could. He'd be totally cool about it. That's the kind of person he was. That's why she liked him so much.

Laura, meanwhile, was on the phone with Mike at breakfast. "We're getting manicures after lunch," she told him, in a flat emotionless voice. "And then, if you wouldn't mind, I thought you could come to my house at five for pictures. That will give you plenty of time to go to Daniel's if you want."

"But you're coming to Daniel's, too. Right?" Mike said into the phone. He was at his own house, eating breakfast.

"If you want, I will—"

"What do you mean, *if I want*?" said Mike. "Of course I want. Those guys are expecting you."

"I just mean if you're going crazy and you can't stand being with us, you can leave."

"I won't go crazy," said Mike, softening his tone.

"Listen. I'm sorry about the tux thing. Of course I want to be with you. It'll be fun. We'll do pictures at your house and then we'll go to Daniel's. Daniel has the limo from six on."

"Okay."

"And we can meet everyone at Alberto's Italian. And don't worry about Daniel and those guys. They want to hang out. They told me to bring all you guys to the Chill Room. To stake out our territory."

"Mike, I have to tell you. I don't want to spend my whole prom night hiding away in some . . . room."

"You don't hang out there all night," said Mike. "You just go there to relax. It'll be dark and cozy. It'll be romantic. That's why we got it."

Laura said nothing.

"Don't worry so much," said Mike. "We're gonna have fun. All right?"

"All right," said Laura, into the phone.

"I love you," said Mike.

"I love you, too," said Laura.

40

On "Prom Friday," Jace and Chloe had no problem sneaking off campus at lunchtime—everyone was skipping classes and sneaking around. The parking lot was so busy there were traffic jams.

Jace drove them to the manicure place where they

were to meet Laura and Abby. Neither Jace nor Chloe felt a great need for a manicure, but everyone insisted this was an essential part of the prom experience.

Barbara's, the place most people went, was booked solid, so Laura had made them all appointments at twelve thirty at a different place called Happy Hands in Weston Heights. It was where the rich old ladies went.

Of course, Chloe had never been to any kind of manicure place. Neither had Jace. They looked through the glass while they waited. Inside, the dozen manicurists wore surgical masks. They worked like little monks, bent over their customers' hands, studying their nails under huge magnifying glasses.

"This looks very weird," said Jace, frowning.

"I hate stuff like this," said Chloe.

"We might as well do it, though," said Jace. "Right?"

"I guess. If it's part of the *prom experience*."

Abby pulled up in her silver Subaru Outback. She was talking on her cell phone. Neither Chloe nor Jace knew Abby very well, though they would do their best to be friends with her now—especially Chloe, who wanted more information about Zach. She started to tell Abby the story of talking to him on the phone, but Abby waved her away. "Don't worry about Zach," she said, cell phone in hand. "He's totally going to like you."

"But how do you know?"

"It's a no-brainer," said Abby.

"But why?"

"Zach is famously eccentric. He once walked around naked in the rain for hours. And he wasn't even on drugs."

Chloe looked at Jace. "What's so great about that?"

"He likes weird people," said Abby. "He's an experimenter."

Chloe made a face. "I'm not an *experiment*."

"In a way you are," said Abby, sweetly. "You guys are going to love each other. Seriously. Don't worry about it."

This did not make Chloe feel better. She and Jace watched Abby dial a new number on her cell phone. "Mom?" she said loudly into her phone. "Hey. I just got here. . . . It's called Happy Hands. . . . I know. . . . It looks okay. There's two Mercedes in the parking lot. . . . No, no, it's fine, it'll be fun."

Jace and Chloe looked through the large window. It didn't look like fun to them.

When Laura arrived, the four girls went in. Abby went first. She was having a manicure and a pedicure. The pedicure was because she was wearing sandals, she explained to Chloe, who had never seen a pedicure before and was alarmed when one of the women began sanding the bottom of Abby's feet.

The other girls were taken to their own stations. Chloe was assigned a tiny Asian woman who grabbed her hands and jammed them in a slimy, oily liquid.

"Jeez, Chloe, don't look so terrified," said Laura from

across the room. "This is supposed to be fun."

Chloe tried to smile. All around her the smell of chemicals was very strong. And though there were fans and air conditioners everywhere, the fact that the workers wore surgical masks obviously meant the chemicals were toxic. Chloe tried to relax and listen to the music. You could barely hear it over all the poison air being blown around. It was lite FM anyway, not Chloe's favorite.

After the soaking, the woman produced a shiny metal poking device and began stabbing the tops of Chloe's fingernails with it. "Oww," said Chloe. "Oww . . . oww . . . OUCH!" She yanked her hand back from the woman. Everyone in the shop turned to look.

"Chloe," hissed Laura, from across the room.

"What? It hurts."

"It's *supposed* to hurt."

"Then why do they do it?" asked Chloe.

"It's like the dentist," said Abby, who had her cell phone out. Abby looked very at-home here, which did not make Chloe like her more.

Meanwhile, the Asian woman gestured for Chloe's arm. She wanted Chloe's hand back.

"What's her problem?" asked Chloe.

"Shhhh," said Abby. "Just let them do it."

Chloe surrendered her hand. The woman resumed stabbing the cuticles. It hurt. Chloe grimaced. She crossed and recrossed her legs. She did not understand the feminine world. She did not understand being a girl. She wished Shawnie and Rebecca were there. Shawnie would never stand for this kind of physical abuse.

When they were finished, the four girls stood squinting in the parking lot. The sun had finally appeared, briefly, through a gap in the clouds. Laura and Abby had hair appointments and drove away. This left Jace and Chloe standing by their car, staring at their hands. With Abby's help, Chloe had selected a "classy," light brown nail polish. Her fingers did look elegant, though to Chloe it was more bizarre than attractive. And the tops of her fingers still hurt. They hurt a lot.

Jace and Chloe, with an hour to kill, decided to splurge and have lunch at the sushi place next door. This turned out to be an unexpected highlight of the day. Of the three original friends, Chloe and Jace probably had the least in common. Unlike Laura, who dutifully kept up with old friends, neither Chloe nor Jace had made a great effort to stay close. And yet, from the moment they sat down, the comfort of their old friendship returned. They talked easily and calmly. Their old selves returned: pre-artsy Chloe, pre-jock Jace. They talked about prom but also about other things—how their lives had changed, what school was like, where they might go to college. By the end of the lunch they both felt thoroughly refreshed by the talk, by the peaceful hour in a deserted sushi place in a neighborhood they never went to.

Unfortunately, when they looked at their watches it was almost three. They had to get home. They had two hours to get dressed and get to Laura's for pictures.

41

Jace dropped Chloe off at home. Chloe hurried inside and immediately fell into a panic. Where was her dress? Where were her shoes? Where was her mother?

Her phone rang almost as soon as she was in the door—Laura checking to see when she was coming over. Chloe didn't know. She had to get ready. She had to shower, get dressed, get her hair ready, put on makeup—though Chloe knew nothing about makeup.

Chloe stripped off her clothes and literally jumped into the shower. She loofahed herself thoroughly, washed her hair, conditioned it, washed her face, then did it all again. She got out, dried off, and blow-dried her hair, though she'd never been good with blow-dryers and afterward her hair stuck up funny on top. Her plastic red barrette would fix that if she was brave enough to wear it. That was the problem now: The Real Chloe vs. a Sanitized Prom Chloe. How unique did she dare be? But you couldn't change yourself, not in thirty-five minutes.

She went into her room and got her dress out of the closet. She spread it on the bed with the sleek black pumps that had mysteriously appeared at the vintage store, and which Brian—thank God—had made her buy. She considered the outfit with a newly critical eye. It would stand out. It would look too fancy. Suddenly, she didn't want to be a vintage retro Audrey Hepburn, she just wanted to be like everyone else. Or did she? It didn't matter; she had no time for a dress debate now. She dug through her underwear drawer. Where were her favorite panties? She ran downstairs and found them in the main hamper—*unwashed*. How could she have forgotten to wash them? And what about the boutonniere for Zach? Her mom was supposed to buy it, but where was it? Where was her mom!?

She ran back upstairs and put on different panties. In the mirror they looked old and frumpy. Laura had told her to buy new underwear and Chloe had not and was now reduced to old underwear, and not even her favorites. Her mother, who had finally come home with the boutonniere, appeared at Chloe's door and volunteered to do a special wash if she needed it. Chloe said no, there was no time, no one was going to see her underwear, anyway.

"But, Chloe," said her mother. "It's about how you feel. . . ."

What Chloe felt was rushed. For various reasons she ran downstairs, upstairs, out to the garage, down to the basement, around the living room, and back up to her room again. And then the doorbell rang. She and her mother glared at each other. *Who could that be?*

Her mother ran downstairs and answered the door. It was Rebecca. What did she want? She just wanted to stop in, say hi, see how things were going.

Mrs. Thomas let her in. Rebecca came upstairs, moving in an odd slow-motion way, completely counter to the frenzied rush of Chloe and her mother. She settled on Chloe's bed while Chloe clumsily, hurriedly tried to apply some eyeliner.

"So I guess you're pretty excited," said Rebecca.

"Excited?" said Chloe. "I'm totally peeing my pants!"

"Well that makes sense, I guess," said Rebecca. "What are you doing?"

"I'm trying to put on eyeliner."

"I don't think that's how you do it."

"Well how *do* you do it?" said Chloe. "Mom!?"

Chloe's mother, who was washing Chloe's underwear despite her daughter's instructions, came back upstairs. But her mother wasn't a big makeup person, either; they both took their turn at it. It didn't look very good.

Chloe shifted her focus on which of her barrettes to wear, where exactly to wear it, and even if she should wear it.

Her mother, meanwhile, tried a little blush on Chloe's cheeks. It made her look like a child prostitute. She tried to scrub it off.

"I can't believe you're going to the prom," murmured Rebecca.

"That's not helping, Rebecca," said Chloe, moving her hands around her mother's in an attempt to adjust her hair.

"Do you have to wear that barrette?" said her mother. "Maybe you should wear your hair down. Like a grown-up."

"People won't know who I am," said Chloe. But she tried it. She let her hair down. Rebecca and her mother both stared at her in the mirror. With her hair down, Chloe looked more sophisticated, more adult, sexier, hotter.

"No, I'm wearing it," said Chloe. She grabbed her hair, pushed it roughly to the side, snapped in the barrette. It looked even nerdier than usual.

While her mom continued to repair the bad makeup job, Rebecca dug through her coat pockets. When Mrs. Thomas left for a moment, Rebecca got up from the bed. "I was wondering if you wanted this," she asked, holding her hand out.

Chloe looked. It was the "Girls Kick Ass" button.

"Just to borrow for the night," said Rebecca.

"That's not really a prom-type concept," said Chloe.

"Yeah, but it's still cool."

"You can't wear buttons on a fancy dress, though, can you?" Chloe took the button and held it against the left side of her dress. She tried it on the other side. She tried it lower down.

"It doesn't really go anywhere," she said.

"Yeah, you're right," admitted Rebecca. "It doesn't really work."

"I wish it did," said Chloe, warming to the idea.

Whoever Zach turned out to be, he might as well deal with her as she was, right from the start.

"How about on your purse?" said Rebecca.

"My purse?" said Chloe.

"You're going to bring a purse, aren't you?"

"I hadn't thought about it."

"You can't bring a backpack," said Rebecca.

"No, you're right."

"So what are you going to put your stuff in?"

"I don't know," said Chloe. *"Mom!?"*

42

Jace was having her own pre-prom troubles at home. For her it was not issues of wardrobe or personal identity. For her it was the problem of living in a house full of very protective males, none of whom were entirely comfortable with the idea that she was going to a prom with a mentally ill, convicted reckless endangerer. Jace had assured everyone that Paul was sane, reasonable, cautious, and safe. Nor would he "try anything," since she and Paul were "just friends." The Torres men remained unconvinced.

"I don't care how nice he is," said her father, who was a foreman for a large construction company. "I want to meet him."

"Me, too," said her oldest brother, who, like her father,

was thick and powerful-looking and could probably crush most teenage boys with one hand.

"And me, too," said her second oldest brother, who looked tougher still, his nose having been broken playing basketball when he was at Evergreen.

"You guys just want to scare him," said Jace, who had seen her dad and brothers do the intimidation routine before. The truth was, the few guys Jace had ever been attracted to were like Paul: smart, thoughtful, shy. In no instance had she liked a boy whom she needed protection from. But the Torres men saw their role as the same in any case. So they hung around the house like sheriff's deputies waiting for Paul to appear.

The other issue was makeup. Jace hated makeup and especially hated when Hispanic women wore too much of it. But her reclusive aunt Maria had been summoned and was waiting for her when she returned from the manicure. Aunt Maria had worked in a beauty shop in Guadalajara for twenty years, and Jace's father thought it a point of family honor that she be included in the preparation process. Jace refused at first. But when she saw how this hurt her aunt, she reluctantly agreed, secretly swearing that if she ended up looking like a *barrio bambina* she would simply shower again and wash it all off. Luckily for her, Aunt Maria showed remarkable restraint, somehow grasping that this mythical Paul Stoyanovich would appreciate elegance over exaggeration. When Aunt Maria was done, Jace looked so stunningly beautiful she did not recognize herself in the mirror. She had to stare at herself for several minutes. Then she had to *stop* looking; it was too weird, too disorienting.

At 4:55 the doorbell rang. Jace—dressed, made-up, manicured, and nauseous with nerves—jumped off the couch and ran to the door. Her brothers got up from the kitchen table. Aunt Maria, hiding in a back hallway, snuck forward and peered around the corner.

Jace opened the door. It was Paul. In an elegant black tuxedo. He stood awkwardly before her, his head bent slightly, holding a dozen white roses. His usually mussed blond hair was neatly combed out of his face, so that his blue eyes shone more brightly than ever. Jace could not take her eyes off him. She knew nothing about tuxedos, but she saw immediately that his was special. It was not a rental. It fit right, it looked right, and Paul's handsomeness set it off brilliantly. He looked like a prince, like a *real* prince. He was the best-looking boy she had ever seen.

"These are for you," he said, handing her the bouquet. "And I have your corsage in the car."

"Oh my . . . God!" Jace gasped. She could barely breath she was so excited. She held out his boutonniere.

"You look . . . *amazing*," said Paul, taking it.

"Ahem," said a thick male voice from inside.

"Oh come in, come in," said Jace, remembering herself. Paul stepped into the house. Jace's father and her brothers had moved themselves into the living room. "Come in and meet my dad," said Jace.

Paul moved into the living room. Jace could see the anxiety in his face, but he quickly covered it with a deep smile.

"Hello, Paul!" said Mr. Torres, with authority.

"Hello, Mr. Torres."

"These are my sons, Carlos, Miguel, and Juan."

"Hi," said Paul. "Nice to meet you all." He shook their hands. It was obvious to everyone that Paul was a perfect gentleman, and the Torres men, without any male threat to contend with, found themselves speechless and slightly embarrassed.

"Congratulations," Carlos managed. "On making the tennis finals."

"Yeah, we read about you . . . I mean . . . we heard about . . ." mumbled Juan.

"Thanks," said Paul. "I wish I could have beat that last guy. It wasn't meant to be, I guess."

"What kind of car you driving?" said Mr. Torres, who, when conversations stalled, could always talk about cars.

"I have my uncle's Suburban."

"Yeah?" said Mr. Torres. He was a big fan of Suburbans—his company used a small fleet of them. He went to the window and looked out. "What year is it?"

"I'm not sure," said Paul. "Maybe last year's?"

Mr. Torres was impressed. He admired it from the window. "I think that's from two years ago," he said.

"Could be," said Paul.

"So, Paul," said Mr. Torres, coming away from the window. "You plan on drinking tonight?"

"No, sir," he said. "That's why my uncle thought I should bring the big car, in case I had to give other people rides. . . ."

"That's a nice plan," said Mr. Torres. "But young people don't always stick to their plans."

"No, I won't be drinking," Paul assured him. "Really, not at all. I can't, doctor's orders. "

"We'll be *fine,* Daddy," said Jace, giving her father a nasty look. "We're supposed to be at Laura's, and we're going to be late."

"All right," said Mr. Torres. A resignation came into his face. He trusted Paul. He was happy for them both. Maybe too happy, thought Jace. He was getting a certain look in his face. That sentimental, I'm-so-happy-I-could-cry look he got on holidays and other family occasions. Jace cringed when she saw it. If her father started *crying* . . .

A bright flash went off. It was Aunt Maria. She had snuck forward, taken a picture, and run back into the hall.

"That's just my crazy aunt," Jace told Paul. "She runs off and hides."

"I see," said Paul, who always liked evidence that other people were as strange as he was.

"We have to go," said Jace. She grabbed Paul's arm and led him toward the door.

Mr. Torres looked out the window at the Suburban

again. Paul's was black. The one he drove was gray, but he liked the black ones.

Jace had Paul out the door and almost to the driveway when her father called for her to stop. "One minute, Julia!" he commanded in his foreman's voice. "Maria, get out here."

Mr. Torres came onto the front lawn. Aunt Maria appeared at the front door. "Get out here and take some pictures," he told her.

"Dad!" protested Jace. "We're late. You can get copies of the pictures from Laura's."

"Maria!" Mr. Torres yelled. "Get out here! Take some pictures!"

Aunt Maria came out of the house. Jace was horrified. "It's okay," whispered Paul.

"But you don't understand," said Jace, gripping Paul's arm. "She's a total freak. She can barely speak English."

Aunt Maria came out with her ancient Kodak Instamatic, and took a picture.

"More!" commanded Mr. Torres. "Smile, Jace! Smile, Paul!" The two did as they were told.

Aunt Maria took four pictures. Then she ran back inside. "See?" said Jace. "She's totally weird. I mean, she's nice and everything. She did my makeup."

"Wait," said Paul. "*She* did your makeup?"

Jace nodded.

"That woman with the camera did your makeup?" repeated Paul.

"Yes, but c'mon, before they do something even more ridiculous."

"Thank you, Aunt Maria!" yelled Paul, turning back toward the house. Jace pulled on his arm. The old woman immediately appeared at the window, waving.

Paul waved back. "Thank you! You're a genius! She looks fantastic!"

Aunt Maria smiled and waved more.

"Come *on!*" said Jace, dragging Paul toward the car.

"But your makeup—it's incredible!"

"I know. But whatever. We have to go!"

43

Mrs. Thomas drove Chloe to Laura's. Chloe had forgotten about her clothes anxieties, the makeup problem, and her hair issues. She was now completely and utterly focused on the terror of meeting Zach.

Mrs. Thomas was also suddenly nervous. She hadn't planned to get involved in the pre-prom photo shoot; Chloe didn't want her to, and—like her daughter—she looked down on people who overdid prom. However, at the last minute, she had slipped her camera into the car, figuring that since she'd be there anyway, surely no one would mind if she took a few pictures.

Another thing: Rebecca was still with them. No one had invited her; she had simply followed them into the car.

Chloe didn't care; she was barely aware of her friend's presence. And Mrs. Thomas wasn't going to tell her to go home.

Chloe sat in the front seat. She didn't move. She didn't speak. She stared forward like she was being driven to an execution. "Are you okay, honey?" said her mother.

Chloe made no reply.

"Look, the sun's coming out," said Rebecca, gazing out the window.

"So, Rebecca," said Mrs. Thomas, needing to talk to someone. "Why aren't you going to the prom?"

"No reason."

"Did you want to go?"

"No, I guess not."

"Why not?"

"I dunno."

Mrs. Thomas signaled and changed lanes.

"You could still go," said Chloe, suddenly breaking her silence.

"No," said Rebecca. "It's better if you go. You can tell me what it's like."

"I don't think it's fair to live your life through me," said Chloe, pointedly. "You should do things for yourself."

No one knew how to take this outburst from Chloe. No one spoke.

On Laura's street, Chloe reached a new pinnacle of panic and self-doubt. Why had she agreed to this? Why had she done this to herself? In a few seconds she would have to leave the car, walk into Laura's house, and begin what would probably be the most humiliating night of her life. She looked terrible. She felt like throwing up. In her lap she held a clunky old purse of her mother's, the "Girls Kick Ass" button stuck on it, which looked moronic. She wore a pretentious dress, ridiculous shoes, a retarded barrette. She had on the wrong underwear. Her hair was sticking up on top. The only thing about her appearance that was even remotely acceptable was her fingernails, and she had already chipped one of those in her kitchen trying to open a bottle of Pepto-Bismol.

The car stopped. They had arrived. Chloe obviously hated herself. It was the only explanation for why she had done this. She opened the door. As she untangled herself from her seatbelt, she heard someone on Laura's front stoop announce her arrival. "She's here! Chloe's here!"

Something about the voice gave Chloe an idea, an intellectual escape route. She would not think of this as her prom. She would think of it as theirs. She would play this as the good soldier. *She was doing this for her friends.* What happened to her was not important. And since nothing good was going to happen, it was best to just grit her teeth, lower her head, slog her way through.

"Zach!" said someone on the front porch. "Hey, Zach! Your date is here!"

Chloe began the death march up the lawn. Her head hung so far down she appeared to be studying the grass. The screen door slammed and a new person—a boy—

appeared. Chloe knew who it was from the whispering all around her. Her head dipped even farther.

"Chloe?" said a male voice, when she'd reached the front steps. Chloe lifted her head just enough to see a pair of white shoes on the top step. Laura and Jace ran down the stairs and grabbed her arms.

"*Chlo*-e!" urged Laura. "Look up! It's Zach!"

Chloe slowly, miserably, raised her head. In front of her, in a white tuxedo, was a tall, hairy, freckly . . . boy. He had so much reddish-brown hair it was almost an Afro. She couldn't really see his face. And why was he dressed all in white? Even his shoes were white. They had little gold bars across the top of them. Chloe looked down at her own feet.

"Chloe, say hi!" said Jace. Abby giggled somewhere. Apparently bets had been made about Chloe's reaction, because someone said, "I told you she'd lose it!"

"All right, c'mon in everyone," said Laura's mother, who appeared suddenly and began pulling the kids inside. She was surprised to see Chloe's mother: "Oh hello, Heidi, I didn't know you were coming."

"Well . . . I wasn't planning to . . . but I happened to have my camera in the car . . . and since I'm here . . ."

"Of course, of course, and who are you, young lady?"

"Rebecca," said Rebecca, rolling her fists up into her military coat sleeves. "I'm just here to watch."

"All right then. Come in, everyone. Come in. Let's take some pictures!"

44

Chloe followed everyone inside. The house was alive with people: Laura's parents, Laura's nana, other parents, neighbors, some stray relatives, some smiling old ladies. Mike and Daniel stood off to the side. Marianne was with them, looking bored. Her slutty friend, Christine, was biting carrots in half at the buffet. Chloe had to move so some gossiping mothers could get around her. Abby was already there. Abby's boyfriend, Eric, was dressed in an outrageous paisley suit. Abby's mother was obvious and easy to spot; she was the punk mom. There were other grown-ups, other kids, Jace and Paul, Betsy Julevitz and her date. Chloe was surprised when she turned and her own mother was there, camera in hand. And even more surprising: Rebecca was still wandering around.

"Chloe?" someone said. Chloe could barely process all the different people, all the different conversations. In the midst of it all Zach was somewhere. She had been rude to him out front; she needed to find him, to say something.

"Chloe?" said the same voice. It was Laura. "Do you have Zach's boutonniere?"

Chloe's stomach tightened. She had forgotten it. Her

mom had bought it, and put it in the fridge, and Chloe had forgotten it.

"Oh, Chloe, you didn't forget it?"

Chloe nodded that she had.

"Someone send her mother back," said a voice.

"Does someone have an extra one?" said another voice.

Chloe wanted to die. Rebecca was found and dispatched to find Mrs. Thomas. Meanwhile, people took pictures, flashes went off. And then, when all hope seemed lost, someone's mother did have an extra boutonniere. It was retrieved and jammed into Chloe's hands. Laura pushed her forward, whispering: "Now give it to Zach, before you lose it. And be nice to him. He's your date!"

Chloe stumbled forward. Zach stood at the buffet with Eric. "Hi, Zach," she managed to say.

"Hey," said Zach, smiling affably. He didn't have an Afro; he just had long, floppy, curly red hair.

"Here's this thing for your coat," said Chloe.

"Thanks," he said. "And I got this corsage for you."

Chloe swallowed. She was sick with nerves. She kept her eyes down as Zach fumbled with the plastic container that held the corsage. He got it open and awkwardly held the flower in the general direction of her chest. Chloe waited for him to put it on her. But how could he, without touching her breast? "Can I help you guys?" said

Abby. She took the corsage and, leading Chloe subtly away, helped her pin it to the front of her dress.

"Chloe, you gotta relax," whispered Abby. "And stop frowning. You look miserable."

Chloe tried a smile, but it felt bizarre on her face. Soon, she would have no choice but to smile. Most of the dates and small group pictures were taken and it was time for the big group finales. Chloe was pushed and prodded until she was in a line with the fifteen other prom-goers who were present. Once the group was gathered, the cameras exploded with flashes, clicks, and whirrs. It was like being lined up and shot, thought Chloe, who could not get the execution metaphor out of her head. Everything they did was like the death of something: their innocence, their youth, their childhood dreams.

"Now, you three girls," someone said. "The Three Ts."

"The Three Ts!" repeated other voices. Chloe found herself alone in front of the cameras with her two best friends from eighth grade, Jace and Laura. Jace, who looked like a movie star, with her expensive dress and precise makeup; Laura, whose natural good looks had suddenly been transformed into a beautiful elegance. Chloe felt utterly wrong beside them, with her "Girls Kick Ass" purse and her dumb barrette. She reached up and tried to tear it out, but Laura's mother scolded her and told her to put her hand down.

"Smile, Chloe Thomas!" another mother commanded.

Chloe did, but with a look of defeat and despair so painfully obvious that many of the parents instantly deleted the image from their digital cameras.

And she still had the whole night to get through.

45

After the pictures, Daniel's limo appeared. It would take Daniel, Mike, Laura, and the other seniors to Daniel's for more pictures, and then on to Alberto's Italian for dinner.

Abby's boyfriend, Eric, pulled behind the limo in his Ford Expedition. Abby, Zach and another couple crawled in. Chloe tried to follow Jace and Betsy into Paul's Suburban, but before they could leave, Abby left Eric's car and came back for Chloe. "Chloe, what are you doing in that car?"

"Riding in it?"

"You're supposed to be in our car. With Zach."

"I thought I was going with—"

Jace pushed her out of the Suburban. Chloe reluctantly followed Abby to Eric's car, though this was exactly what *wasn't* supposed to happen. She was supposed to be with Jace and Laura. Now the three of them were in different cars. *Girls always do what boys want,* thought Chloe. She followed Abby to Eric's car. She wondered if her mom would protest her riding with people she didn't know, but her mother was now lost among the fawning adults who continued to sigh and take pictures and gush among themselves.

As Chloe climbed into the Expedition, she spotted Rebecca, standing at the top of Laura's lawn. Rebecca stood by herself, watching, unnoticed. Chloe wondered if maybe she *had* done the right thing. At least Chloe hadn't chickened out; at least when it was over she would have been through something. She would be a slightly different person than when it started. She waved to Rebecca, who saw her and waved back, still in that regretful slow motion she'd maintained all afternoon.

"Get in," said Eric. "Come on, you guys."

Chloe took her place in the middle of the backseat, Zach to her left, Abby to her right.

They began to drive. Chloe sat without speaking, afraid to look at Zach. "So how's it going?" Zach finally asked her.

"Okay," said Chloe, attempting cheerfulness. "How's it going with you?"

"Okay."

When no one talked, Chloe glanced awkwardly into Zach's face and said, "I wrote thirty-one poems about you."

Abby jabbed her in the ribs with her elbow. *"Chloe!"* she hissed.

"What?" whispered Chloe.

"Don't be *weird.*"

Zach, if he heard this, ignored it. "What kind of poems?" he asked.

"Not really about you *specifically*," explained Chloe, bracing herself against Abby. "Just about, you know, blind dates and imagining people you haven't met yet. You know, the mystery factor."

"The mystery factor," said Zach, nodding. "That's cool."

"I like your tux. It's white."

"Duh," whispered Abby beside Chloe.

"Yeah, it's my brother's," said Zach. "I like your dress."

"I know, I got it at this vintage store downtown. There was this crazy lady who smoked—"

"Yeah? Was it called Retread Threads?"

"It was!" said Chloe.

"I know that place," said Zach, smiling. "It's on Alder; it's, like, totally jammed with crap. . . ."

"Totally, and the lady chain-smokes."

"Yeah," said Zach. "The crazy lady."

"Where'd you get those shoes?" Chloe asked.

"At a Salvation Army in Gresham. They were four bucks."

Chloe looked down at his shoes. She looked back at his face. Under his hair, Zach had soft, green eyes. And his skin was milky-white, red in the cheeks, with freckles.

Eric cranked the stereo. Chloe was glad for the distraction. She sat back and moved her head to the beat. Abby grinned with amusement. *I told you,* she silently mouthed to Chloe.

What? mouthed Chloe.

That you would like him, she mouthed.

Chloe didn't want to admit that she liked anyone at this point. But she was beginning to relax a little. She was starting to have fun.

46

Laura had never been in a limo before. Daniel had, a fact he seemed determined to prove to everyone by demonstrating every available gadget. He opened the sunroof, ran the tinted windows up and down, turned on the interior lights, and showed everyone how to use the CD player. He equalized the music and helped himself to the minibar. Of course there was no alcohol in it, but Daniel had a flask of something in his tux coat pocket, so that wasn't a problem. Marianne lit a cigarette in the limo, which Laura was surprised you could do. Laura hoped no one started smoking pot. She didn't want the smell to get on her dress.

Laura also felt the nagging suspicion that if she were not present, people would be making fun of her house and family. Daniel's parents were rich, she knew; his dad was a lawyer. Mike's parents were comfortable, golf-club types. Marianne's parents she didn't know anything about; they were probably not so great, since Marianne had smoked cigarettes since she was a freshman, among other things.

"Hey, that was sorta fun," said Mike, as if reading Laura's mind.

"What was?" said Marianne.

"Taking pictures."

"Oh. You thought so?" said Laura.

"Sure," said Mike who had been oddly attentive to her at her parents' house. He was making an extra effort, which was good, but for some reason, Laura didn't trust it.

"I love your grandmother," said Marianne, smoking her cigarette. "What did you call her, your *nana*?"

Laura nodded. She didn't want to talk to Marianne about her nana.

"You always complain about your parents," Mike said to Laura. "But they're okay." He squeezed her around the waist as the limo turned a corner. He leaned over and kissed her on the cheek.

"Jesus, you two," teased Marianne. "Get a room."

"We got a room," Daniel reminded everyone. "The Chill Room. Seniors only. And their dates, of course."

Everyone chuckled at that. Laura smiled and sat back on the plush limousine upholstery. She thought back to her first prom. How perfect Mike had been, how patient, and loving, and giving. They were so in love that night, like nothing she had ever felt. What were they now? In love still? Or after a certain point was it more about the other parts of a relationship? The trust, the consistency. It was like being married, having a boyfriend for over a year.

Marianne lowered her window and flicked an ash out. Daniel played with the stereo. "Jesus, Daniel," said Marianne. "Act like you've been in a limo before."

"I'm just showing everyone."

"I'm sure we all know how to put a CD in a CD player," said Marianne. "What music did you bring, anyway?"

"I got a couple things," said Daniel. "Some Linkin Park . . ."

"Linkin *Park*?" sneered Marianne, smoking her cigarette. Her slinky dress barely contained her large and surprisingly tanned breasts. To Laura she seemed so much older, so much more *womanly* than other Evergreen girls. Even the way she smelled, and the way her skin was already rough and textured. She was certainly too cool for Daniel, which she was making very clear at the moment.

"Why didn't you tell me you wanted different music?" Daniel asked her.

"I can't tell you everything."

"If you want, we can stop and buy something." He held up a phone. "You call the driver on this thing. He'll take us wherever we want to go."

They didn't stop. They went to Daniel's and pulled into his long circular driveway. The Weiss house was a sleek, modern ranch house nestled into three acres of woods. Laura had been there for Daniel's legendary Christmas party. That was when he and Marianne first hooked up.

Or at least when Marianne decided Daniel was the person she wanted to sleep with and make fun of for the final semester of her high school career.

Laura had been expecting a repeat of the photo event at her house, but no one appeared to be home at Daniel's. She followed the others inside. Marianne instantly ditched her corsage, which was irritating her for some reason. She threw it in the sink. Mike and Daniel loosened their bow ties and opened beers. Marianne and Christine and Christine's silent date, Dirk, went straight to the fridge and helped themselves to a bottle of champagne. It took some doing, but the top finally popped out. No champagne poured out like the movies, though. They offered some to Laura, who took a skinny glass. She took a couple sips, though she was not a huge fan of "the bubbly."

Finally, Daniel's mother appeared. She was dressed in a bathrobe and slippers. "Look at you guys, look how cute you are!" she said, though she made no movement to record the moment with pictures.

Daniel, Dirk, and Mike disappeared upstairs for a moment, and Marianne poured Mrs. Weiss some champagne. The four women all held up their champagne glasses. "To men!" said Daniel's mother, and everyone laughed. Then Marianne and Christine went looking for something in the limo, and Laura found herself alone with Mrs. Weiss. The two made small talk. Mrs. Weiss poured herself some more champagne and took a seat on one of the bar stools. She crossed her legs in a sophisticated pose, exposing one of her legs to the top of the thigh. Suddenly, Daniel's attraction to Marianne made more sense.

Fifteen minutes later they were all back in the limo. Mike again was helpful and attentive, kissing Laura on the forehead and checking that she was okay.

"What were you guys doing upstairs?" Laura asked, as they settled in their seats.

"Nothing. Daniel had to refill his flask."

Laura nodded.

"Don't worry, this is going to be a great prom."

"I hope so," said Laura.

47

Laura felt better when they arrived at Alberto's Italian. Paul and Jace were standing outside when they pulled up. They both looked amazing, like movie stars, Laura thought. They were going to have a fantastic night.

Everyone went inside. They had reserved the big table in back, and they assembled themselves around it. Here, Laura took control and made sure that she, Jace, and Chloe were at least in talking range. Once that was settled the real fun of prom began, which for Laura was watching Jace and Chloe laugh and goof around and feel the thrill of the night to come. She knew people criticized her for always taking charge of things, but the truth was, helping your friends, creating fun situations, and giving a little push at just the right moment—that was the real joy of life. It was for Laura, anyway.

There was one oversight, though: Zach ended up seated far down the table, away from Chloe. No one seemed to know how to fix this. Abby started to move people around, but it was too complicated and she gave up. In the meantime, Jace, Betsy, and Chloe had giggling fits about various things, including the semi-naked people painted on the wall of Alberto's back room. There were nymphs and Roman gods and a goat, all of which were hilariously funny for some reason. Mike and Daniel repeatedly got up and went to the restroom. It occurred to Laura that they were doing cocaine but she didn't feel any desire to investigate. Also, Marianne and Christine were sneaking something into their Sprites. *Whatever*, thought Laura. Paul sat across from her so she enjoyed looking at him during the appetizers. He was so handsome, and so nice, sitting there, smiling to himself, totally enjoying Jace and happy she was having so much fun.

"Do you think Zach's cute?" Chloe whispered to Jace. The food had arrived. Nobody was very hungry, though.

"He seems cute," said Jace. "It's hard to tell with all that hair."

"I saw his face in the car," said Chloe, chomping on a breadstick. "He has green eyes."

"I like his white tux," interjected Betsy. "You know he has a sense of humor."

"Thank God he does," Abby whispered, joining in. "You should have seen Chloe in the car. The first thing she said to him was 'I wrote thirty-one poems about you'!"

The girls gasped.

"He didn't care," said Chloe, without worry. "I told him they weren't about him *specifically*."

"You're lucky," said Abby. "I think he likes you."

"How could he?" said Chloe. "He doesn't even know me."

"Maybe you should take off that barrette," said Laura, reaching across the table.

"No!" said Chloe, pushing her hand away. "If he's going to like me, he can like me with my barrette."

"What's going on down there?" yelled Zach, from the other end of the table. He threw a roll the length of the table and hit Chloe on the side of the head. Chloe's mouth opened wide and she turned, grabbed a breadstick, and threw it wildly back at him.

Zach ducked as the breadstick bounced off the wall. "Watch out, Zach," said Abby. "You don't want to make Chloe mad."

"Chloe kicks," warned Jace.

"Chloe *kicks ass*," said someone else.

"I'm not afraid of Chloe," came a confident-sounding Zach. "I don't wanna get left out of the fun!"

At that point, chairs were scooted around and Zach and Eric moved down the table so they could more easily throw things at Abby and Chloe. Mike and Daniel and

Marianne and Christine migrated in the other direction so they could sneak to the restroom more easily, and spike their drinks in peace.

48

By eight, the Evergreen party of sixteen—between their food-throwing, their drink-spilling, their plate-swapping and chair-shifting—had successfully trashed the back room at Alberto's Italian. They did leave a very good tip, though, mainly because Daniel was not paying attention and left an extra twenty by mistake.

Paul and Jace were the first out of the restaurant. The sun was setting over the mountains, coloring the sky with soft reds and pinks. Paul unlocked Jace's door. Her smooth skin seemed softer, lovelier in the fading light. Paul hesitated a moment, watching her get in.

Chloe, Zach, and Eric came out a minute later. They were laughing, shouting, teasing one another. They crawled into Eric's car.

Mike, Laura, Daniel, and their group were next. Daniel insisted the limo driver pull directly in front and open their door for them.

Paul and Jace watched the poor limo driver. They were still waiting for Betsy and her date.

"Is Laura okay?" Paul asked Jace. "She looks a little out of place with those people."

"She's gone out with Mike for a year."

"I guess she's used to it."

"Are *you* having fun?" asked Jace.

Paul grinned. "Sure. I'm having a great time."

"Will the prom be okay? It might be pretty crowded."

"I'll be fine," said Paul.

"If you feel weird just tell me," said Jace. "We can always go for a walk or even leave if you want."

"I wouldn't make you leave your prom," scoffed Paul. "What kind of friend do you think I am?"

Jace thought for a moment. "Paul, you're not just my friend, you're my date. We're in this together."

"Yeah, but . . . if I had to leave for some reason . . ."

"Then I would leave, too," insisted Jace.

"But what if you're having fun? What if you meet someone and you want to stay?"

"What are you talking about?" said Jace. "I'm not going to *meet* anyone. You're my date. I'm with you."

"Well," said Paul, avoiding the issue by looking into his side mirror. "I'm sure it'll be no problem."

Jace pressed him: "Do you *want* me to meet someone?"

"No, of course not. But I thought you wanted this to be . . . romantic. That's what you said."

"I do want that," said Jace.

Paul frowned. He adjusted his side mirror. "But you know I can't . . ."

"Can't what?" asked Jace.

Paul sighed. "Listen. I'm glad we're doing this. I'm

sure it'll be great. But when it's all over. It's not like I can . . . you know . . . be your boyfriend or anything."

Jace stared at him indignantly. "Did I say anything about you being my boyfriend?"

"No. But it just seems like . . ."

"Like what?"

"Like that's something you might be thinking about."

Jace didn't answer.

"And that's why I want to be up-front about it," said Paul. "It's not that I don't like you. I do. I totally do. But going out with someone. That's just . . . that's not something I can do right now. It's too soon. I'm not ready—"

There was a knock on the back door. It was Betsy and her date. Jace still had a few things to say in response. But it would have to wait. She managed a smile as she unlocked the door and let Betsy in.

49

With car stereo blasting, Eric steered his Ford Expedition into the parking garage at the downtown Hilton. Chloe, sitting between Abby and Zach, stared wide-eyed at the crush of Evergreen students standing at the hotel entrance. The dresses, the tuxedos, the hairstyles; people had been transformed. The most ordinary students were suddenly glamorous and beautiful. It looked like the Oscars of high school.

But they were still gawky kids. In front of them a girl slipped and fell getting out of an SUV. Several girls raced to her rescue, but the fallen girl now had a huge gray smear down the side of her beige dress. At the sight of it, she threw her damaged corsage down and burst into tears.

Other people yelled, waved, frantically ran from group to group. One tuxedoed boy hopped after another tuxedoed boy who had somehow stolen his shoe. Adding to the confusion were parents trying to take last-minute pictures, multiple cell phone conversations, the constant squealing of girls finding their friends and seeing their dresses for the first time.

Holy shit, thought Chloe as she watched the pandemonium.

Eric eased forward and began circling upward into the parking garage in search of a space. On every level prom-goers stood around their cars, boys brushing the fronts of their tuxes, girls adjusting corsages or tugging on the tops of their dresses. A homely girl was touching up her makeup in the side mirror of a Ford pickup truck. Chloe could feel these images emblazoning themselves on her brain. It was true what they said: She would remember this night for the rest of her life.

On the fourth floor, Eric found Paul's Suburban and parked beside it. Jace and Betsy were just getting out. The girls all checked one another's hair and makeup. The boys joked and kidded around. When everyone was ready, they crossed the oily concrete and proceeded down the cement stairwell. On the second floor they encountered three junior boys in tuxedos and trucker caps drinking cans of Pabst Blue Ribbon beer. Everyone said hi and stepped around them. The juniors lifted their beer cans in tribute.

On the ground floor, most of the crowd had moved inside. Chloe and the others followed the arrows that said, "Evergreen Prom." They passed through sliding glass doors and found themselves in a muffled hallway, on a thick red carpet. Fifty feet later they were at the registration table. They signed in and stood in a thick crowd of other couples at the entrance.

This was it. This was the prom. Chloe looked around at the other people. Paul and Jace stood in front of her. Laura and Mike had just arrived and were behind her to the right. She saw Abby take Eric's arm. Other girls took the arms of their dates. She cautiously slipped her hand inside Zach's arm. He did not seem to mind.

"Are you guys ready?" Abby whispered, as the crowd began to move into the ballroom.

Chloe nodded, though the truth was she could barely keep her heart from fluttering out of her chest. She swallowed and tentatively gripped Zach's polyester elbow with her sweaty hand.

Slowly, she shuffled forward with the others, into her high school prom.

50

The grand entrance turned out to be not so grand. Just inside the main room, some nervous person had knocked over a punch bowl. Several girls had been splattered. People were freaking out. Parents ran for mops. It was a mess.

Jace and Paul managed to get around the accident and slip inside the ballroom. Then they ran into Doug Rotter and some tennis players. When they saw Paul they lit up.

"Paul! Hey! What's up?" said Doug.

"Congratulations!" said his friend.

"Thanks," said Paul modestly.

"You did pretty good against Chris Norton," said Doug. "I couldn't win a game off him last year."

Jessica, Doug's girlfriend, turned to Jace. "You look amazing," she said. "Who did your makeup?"

"My aunt," said Jace. She returned the compliment but she wanted to keep moving. She didn't want Paul to get stuck in a crowd of tennis players.

"How's it feel to finish second in state?" they asked Paul.

"It feels good, I guess," said Paul, blushing.

"Is it true you were ranked number one in California once?"

"No, no . . ." said Paul.

"You guys!" said Jace interrupting the conversation. "Can I steal Paul for a sec? We gotta find our friends."

"Sure, okay."

Jace dragged Paul away. She led him through the tables along the dance floor. But everywhere she went the same thing happened. People greeted Paul. Not in a bad way, mostly it was with admiration. Girls cooed, "Hi, Paul." Guys nodded their heads with respect. Everyone had read the article. And they knew he'd gone to the finals at state. And of course he was handsome as hell. Jace couldn't find a place to land. Finally she saw an empty table. She steered Paul to it and sat him down.

"Thanks for getting me away from those guys," he said.

Jace nodded. Now that they were alone, she wanted to finish the conversation they had started in the car. But people kept coming up to them. Two senior girls appeared. They tapped Paul on the shoulder. "Hey, Paul," they said. "We just want to say we think it's awesome you almost won state," they said. "Good luck."

"Thanks," said Paul.

The girls left. Jace watched them go but then fell silent. She stared at the empty dance floor, unable to face him.

"Jace?" said Paul. "Are you okay?"

"Of course," she said, faking a smile.

He touched her arm. "What is it? Is it what I said at the restaurant?"

Jace didn't answer.

"Hey, I didn't mean for that to ruin your night."

"I know," said Jace.

"I just think we should be honest about things. Don't you?"

"Yes," said Jace. She hesitated. "But that's the thing. Are you really being honest?"

"What do you mean?"

"I mean, if you don't like me at all, why did you even come tonight?" said Jace.

"I didn't say I don't like you at all."

"Then why are you saying all this stuff about how you couldn't go out with someone? And how you're not *ready*?"

"I said it because it's the truth. And I thought I needed to say it."

"It just sounds like . . . an excuse . . . or something you say to get rid of someone."

"Well, it's not," said Paul.

"I mean, if you don't like me that way, just say so. I can take it."

"But I do like you that way. Which is exactly why I don't want to let you down. Or hurt you. I can't do that. I *won't* do that. Doesn't that make sense?"

Jace shook her head slowly. "Not really. Not to me."

Paul sighed. He sat back. "See? This is exactly what I'm talking about. Now I've wrecked your whole night. Everything I do, it always goes bad somehow."

"But why do you act like it's a decision?" said Jace. "Like it's your choice? It's not a choice. People can't help who they like."

"I have to help it," said Paul.

"See? I don't believe that, either."

"Well, if you don't believe anything I say . . ." said Paul.

A slow song had started. A handful of smiling couples strode onto the dance floor in tuxedos and prom dresses. Jace watched them.

"So now what do we do?" asked Paul. "Just argue all night?"

Jace said nothing.

"I shouldn't have even come," said Paul.

"Maybe we shouldn't talk about it right now," said Jace, quietly.

Paul watched her.

"Maybe we should just dance."

51
~

It took about five minutes for Laura to lose Mike. They walked in together, talked to some people together, then she turned and he was gone.

She expected as much and had already made up her mind she would not let Mike's running back and forth to the Chill Room affect her evening. He could run around all he wanted. The fact that they were missing the first slow dance was a little distressing. Still, not that many people were dancing—only about fifteen couples. Most people were still coming in. Laura found Abby and Chloe and the others at one of the tables. They were getting punch, getting settled. Laura did the same.

The dance floor remained mostly empty for several more songs. Then OutKast came on, and, like a dam bursting, the entire student body poured onto the dance floor. Laura let herself be pulled along.

At first she stayed near Zach and Chloe and tried to dance with them. That turned out to be difficult. Zach was a complete lunatic. He grabbed Chloe and spun her swing-dance style. On the third swing, he whipped her so hard she crashed into Eric and Abby and almost knocked them over. Zach then broke into a Russian kick-dance, an Irish jig, and finally a robot dance, which cracked everyone up and earned him a circle of spectators and wild applause. Even Laura couldn't stop laughing.

Then Eric jumped into the circle. He did his own goofy robot dance, complete with "popping," break-dancing, and a bad moonwalk. Then he attempted some floor spin moves, which he couldn't do. It was still fun to watch, though—for everyone but the senior boy who accidentally got kicked in the crotch.

The next song was "Let's Get It Started" by the Black Eyed Peas. People went crazy. The entire ballroom began to bounce to the beat. Betsy and her date had found their way to the center where Chloe and Zach were—not that anyone was dancing together, there was such a mash of people that it was impossible. Paul and Jace were there, too. Zach had settled into a disco shuffle while Chloe whipped her hair around, and made odd arty motions with her arms. Abby and Eric, meanwhile, were practically having sex. Eric was grinding Abby from behind, while she reached around and grabbed his ass. Eventually a chaperone—someone's mom—fought her way through the dance floor to stop them. But this only inspired more people to join in, and soon there was a long train of people grabbing and groping one another.

After half an hour of fast songs there was another slow dance. With Mike still gone, Laura retreated to the table. She drank some punch. In the crowd she spotted Jace. She had lost Paul and in a panic pushed through the other dancers. When she found him, he was alone, looking for her, as desperate as she was. The relief on both their faces warmed Laura's heart. She watched with satisfaction as the two fell into each other's arms and began the slow, turning, dream-walk of the slow-dance.

Laura sat back and watched other couples. Zach and Chloe stood to the side, arguing about something. Abby and Eric slow-danced. Betsy and her date were half-talking, half-dancing. Laura saw other people, people she didn't know well—an old lab partner, a girl whose locker used to be next to hers. These people were not as lucky as

Laura. They had never been in love, they hadn't had boyfriends, many had never had sex. Now they moved slowly, back and forth, their arms around boys they probably liked, boys they probably wanted to go out with.

Laura sipped her punch and remembered what it was like. First dates, first proms, first kisses. It felt bittersweet to be so ahead of people in that way. To have already known the fun they were going to know. But it also made her feel worldly and wise, and like she had something to offer people, like she could teach them—which was something Laura was always eager to do.

52

Mike returned. Laura found him at one of the registration tables near the entrance. He was asking one of the chaperones about the ballots for Prom King and Queen. Laura had forgotten about that. People had downplayed it because last year's Prom King had made a weird speech, insulting his ex-girlfriend and embarrassing everyone. Also, it was traditional that the winners were seniors, and so most of the voting was done by seniors. Still, when Mike handed her a ballot, Laura felt obligated to think about who to vote for. The only boy she could think of was Pat Mulcahy, the captain of the football team. And maybe Sarah Vandeway for the girls because she was so pretty.

"Aren't you going to vote for me?" said Mike.

Laura smiled. "Of course I am, I was trying to choose which girl to write in." She looked to see who Mike had voted for and saw that he had written himself in for the boys. "You're trying for Prom King?" she said.

Mike shrugged. "Sure, why not? Who else is there?"

That was a good question. Mike was as popular in his way as Pat Mulcahy. But if he won Prom King, he'd be stuck with a Prom Queen, someone other than Laura, unless they voted her Prom Queen, which she knew they never would. She wasn't popular enough and she wasn't a senior.

"Write yourself in for Prom Queen," said Mike. "Look, I'm writing you in."

Laura was not the kind of person who wrote herself in. But she wanted to be a good girlfriend. She wrote Mike Gardner in for Prom King and Sarah Vandeway for Prom Queen. It would probably be Pat Mulcahy, anyway.

They handed in their ballots. Laura asked Mike to come dance.

"Why don't you come check out the Chill Room?"

"We can do that later. Everyone's dancing. That guy Zach is doing the robot."

"But at least come check it out," insisted Mike. "It's a real VIP lounge. There's, like, aftershave in the bath-rooms."

Laura gave in and went with him. They walked through all the people at the entrance, out the main doors, out into the hallway, where several parents were stationed to keep an eye on things. Until that moment, Laura had enjoyed the tradition and wholesomeness of what prom represented. She liked how passersby and onlookers smiled at her in her prom dress. Even guests in the hotel seemed happy to have such an event in their vicinity, despite the fact that it clogged the parking lot and filled their lobby with teenagers.

Walking to the Chill Room, that feeling faded. It was as if the other guests understood the difference between people who spent their prom dancing and people who spent their prom in some upstairs lounge, looking down on their classmates. She thought people were staring at her funny. One of the parents seemed to frown. Why was she doing this? The dancing was in the ballroom. Her friends were in the ballroom. The fun was in the ballroom. What was upstairs? Daniel and Marianne making fun of everybody.

"You know what?" Laura said to Mike. "I want to go back to the ballroom."

Mike was thinking about something else. "Wait. Why—"

Laura walked away. She wouldn't look at him. He caught up to her. "Laura, what is it? What's the matter?"

"I just want to have fun tonight. I don't want to go up there."

"We'd only stay a few minutes. You can freshen up or whatever."

"Freshen up?"

"You know, do girl stuff. Marianne and those guys are up there."

"Since when have I ever wanted to hang out with Marianne?"

"But that's why we arranged it. So we'd have our own space."

"I don't need my own space. I want to be with my friends." She started walking again.

Mike grabbed her. He swung her around. "Laura, why are you being like this?"

Laura felt an unexpected sadness pass through her. It ran like a cold wave through her entire body. "Mike, if you want to go, that's fine. You like to party more than I do. You always have. That's fine. I've never minded. But this is a special night for me and I don't want to miss any of it."

Mike swallowed. Whatever had struck Laura seemed to hit him, too. He looked sad and confused. "I still love you, you know," he said. "I know things have felt . . . out of sync or whatever. But I still want you to have a great time."

Laura straightened herself and lifted her eyes to meet Mike's eyes. "Then let me be with my friends. And if you want to go upstairs, then go. It's fine with me. Really, it is."

"Okay," said Mike. "I'll be down in like twenty minutes, *ten* minutes."

"I'll see you then," said Laura.

53

Under normal circumstances Chloe Thomas did not "get her groove on." She did not "shake her booty." She did not "get the party started." Nor did she laugh hysterically, act silly around boys, let herself be picked up, spun around, dipped, or dropped (as had happened twice already). She was, in short, not used to the kind of physical exertion she was engaged in on the dance floor. After an exhausting hour, she had no choice but to get a big glass of punch and collapse in a chair next to Abby. Zach continued to dance. He had completely sweat through his tux and now stood in front of the DJ playing air guitar. Chloe thought he looked ridiculous. He was an embarrassment, a freak, and totally fearless. She liked him.

Then, while Chloe drank her punch, something very unexpected happened. Rebecca said hi to her. Chloe was used to Rebecca sneaking up on her, appearing beside her in odd places. Rebecca didn't like to make a big show of herself. She was the definition of a wallflower.

"Hi, Chloe," she said, again.

Chloe turned in her chair. Rebecca stood behind her. With Brian. Rebecca was at the prom. Rebecca was wearing *a dress*.

"Oh . . . my . . . God," said Chloe, who was too shocked to stand up.

Brian grinned. "We had to. How could we not?"

"Oh my God, it's so beautiful in here," said Rebecca, gazing up at the lofty ceilings.

Chloe nodded that it was, though she herself had not taken any notice of the ballroom.

"Oh great," interrupted Brian. "There's that lady."

"What lady?" said Chloe.

"The lady who saw us come in through the back," said Brian. He pushed Rebecca down into a chair and crouched down beside her.

"You guys snuck in?"

"They wouldn't let us in the front," said Rebecca. "We weren't registered."

Chloe didn't see anyone. But Brian wasn't taking any chances. He crawled under the table, dragging Rebecca down with him. They disappeared under the red tablecloth, which fortunately reached nearly to the floor.

Chloe didn't want to get left out of this adventure. She waited until some girls moved in front of her, slipped off her chair, and crawled under the table, too. It was surprisingly spacious there. It was like a fort when you were a little kid. Chloe scooted toward Rebecca, who was wearing a very cute vintage dress. "Where did you get that?" asked Chloe.

"I had it," said Rebecca.

"Why don't you ever wear it?"

"I never thought to," said Rebecca.

Brian lifted one end of the tablecloth and peeked out.

"What about you?" asked Rebecca. "Have you been dancing?"

"Are you kidding?" said Chloe. "I'm sweating like a pig."

Rebecca leaned closer to her friend. "How is Zach?"

"Oh my God, he is *so* funny."

"He is? Really?"

Chloe nodded.

"But how is he, you know, do you think you could like him? Does he like you?"

Chloe grew serious. "I can't think about that. He tried to dip me and he dropped me on my ass. I'm going to have the biggest bruise."

There was a rustling at the other end of the tablecloth. The group turned in horror as it lifted up.

"Chloe?" said a voice. It was Zach. His large head appeared, upside down.

"What?" said Chloe.

"What are you doing?"

"I'm talking to my friends."

"Oh," said Zach. He looked at the three of them. "Why are you under the table?"

"We just are, all right?"

Rebecca slapped Chloe's leg as if to say, *Don't be mean to him.*

"Okay," said Zach. "Uhm. How long do you think you'll be down there?"

"Not too long."

"Okay," he said. He looked at Brian. "Do you guys want any punch or anything?"

"Nah, we're good," said Brian.

"Okay," said Zach. He dropped the tablecloth back down.

Brian grinned at Chloe. "So that's Zach?"

Chloe nodded.

"I like him," said Brian. "He's got panache."

"What's *panache*?" asked Rebecca.

"It means he doesn't freak out when he finds his prom date under a table."

54

Jace and Paul, after dancing with Chloe and Zach, had eventually moved away from their friends and were now by themselves on the far side of the ballroom. They had drifted there in a slow-dance, and now, as they waited for the next song, Jace stood close to Paul, one finger tucked into the pocket of his vest. Paul slipped his hand around her waist.

There was no next song. Instead, the PA system popped and crackled and someone began talking. It was Bethany Krantz, the prom committee chairperson.

"Hi everyone . . . check . . . check," said Bethany, touching the mike. "Is everyone having a great prom!?"

Several people cheered, "Yes!"

"We *were*," said someone in the back. People laughed.

"Awesome!" said Bethany. "Now I just need to make a couple of announcements."

When it was clear this was going to take a minute, Paul and Jace went back to the group table. Paul left Jace with Chloe and went to get punch. Jace grabbed a chair and found herself sitting next to Rebecca Anderson. That was a surprise. Rebecca wore a not-very-promlike dress. But she seemed extremely excited to be there. Jace squeezed her hand, and the two girls grinned at each other.

Bethany read the license number of a Honda Accord that had its lights on. There was an announcement about the cleanup committee. Also, someone had found an unidentified purse in the girls' bathroom full of money and, according to Bethany, "some things of the latex variety." Everyone thought that was very funny.

"And now the real reason I am up here," she said finally. "We have the voting results of the Prom King and Queen."

This news provoked assorted squeals and groans. Jace had forgotten about the Prom Royalty thing. But she could tell from the reaction of the people around her that this was considered important. She settled herself and waited to hear who it would be.

"Normally," said Bethany, into the microphone, "as most of you know, the Prom King and Queen are seniors. That's the tradition. However, that is not written in stone anywhere, and as a result, we have a little surprise this year."

There were snickers here and there. People looked around the room. Jace noticed several people looking at her table. She immediately thought of Mike. If he won King, then the surprise would be Laura being his Queen, even though she was a junior. That would be exciting, and it made perfect sense. Mike and Laura were one of the longest ongoing couples at Evergreen.

Anyway, it was fun to think about. Who would win? Jace had no clue.

55

Laura, on the other hand, was not terribly interested in who the Prom Queen would be. Laura stood with Abby at the punch table as Bethany talked about the significance of Prom Kings and Queens in a lame attempt to build suspense. Abby got bored and went looking for Eric. Laura scanned the room for Mike. She couldn't find him, but it didn't matter. All sorts of other interesting things were happening: Chloe and Zach getting crazy on the dance floor, Paul and Jace slow-dancing by themselves, the unexpected appearance of Brian Haggert and Rebecca Anderson. That was the real shocker. Rebecca, who was even weirder than Chloe, standing there in a dress. She wasn't exactly a *dress* kind of girl. And she was possibly the worst dancer in the entire ballroom. And yet her presence seemed to mean something to people—Laura wasn't sure what, a victory for the nerds maybe. Anyway, Laura was learning an important lesson. She had thought prom was about being with particular people: your boyfriend, your best friends. This prom seemed to be the opposite: it was about being with everyone. It was about the largest possible group. It was—not to get too corny—about your entire school. Seeing Rebecca in her dress, joining the group, in her reluctant but heartfelt way, was perhaps the most touching thing about the night so far.

Just in time for the crownings, Mike appeared. He had been hiding the coke and alcohol all night. Now it was obvious. His eyes were bloodshot and his speech was scattered and sloppy. His plan was to "party" tonight and that's what he had done.

"Hey there," he said, slipping a hand around Laura's shoulder. When he saw Bethany onstage, he laughed and let go. "I'm not going to win Prom King," he told Laura. "But you know what? I don't care. It's just a popularity contest. You can't win it anyway unless you're student council president. Or you get paralyzed or something."

Laura looked sideways at him.

"Whatever," he said, sliding his hands in his pants pockets and looking around the room. "I don't give a shit."

• • •

Bethany continued her Prom Queen buildup. Laura noticed several people staring at Chloe's table. Chloe and Jace sat with Zach and Abby. Why were people watching them?

She saw Paul making his way through the crowd toward Jace and Chloe. He carried two cups of punch. People congratulated him, patted him on the shoulder as he passed. He didn't look too happy about it, but he smiled his bashful smile. No wonder Jace was so into him. A guy that good-looking, that nice, who was sweet and humble and not a jerk like . . . well, she glanced across at Mike. He was sitting now, staring sullenly forward at the podium. Bethany continued her prom chatter. "Jesus, get on with it," said Mike. "Who's the frickin' Prom King?"

56

Chloe figured it out first. She saw where people were looking. Especially the seniors. They were looking at her table. They were looking at Jace. But they were looking *for* Paul Stoyanovich.

"Jace!" Chloe whispered across the table. But she couldn't get Jace's attention. Jace was too busy wondering why everyone in the entire ballroom was staring at her.

"And this year's Evergreen High School Prom Queen is . . ." said Bethany. "Sarah Vandeway!"

People yelled and clapped. Sarah Vandeway blushed and stood up and did her best to seem surprised. No one was surprised.

"Jace!" said Chloe, again.

But Jace did not hear. She was looking for Paul.

"And this year's Evergreen High School Prom King is . . ." said Bethany.

People started whistling. People started whooping. Chloe grabbed Jace's arm across the table. "Jace, it's—"

"Paul Stoyanovich!"

There was a great cheer in the room and wild applause. Jace turned wildly around in her chair. Paul? *Paul?* Paul was Prom King? How could that be? He was a junior. Juniors couldn't be Prom King. And where was he?

"Jace!" said several people at once. "Jace! *Jace!* Where's Paul!?"

"I don't know," she cried to the dozens of faces that were now intently focused on her.

"Find him!"

"Get him!"

"He's the Prom King!"

Betsy—like a good doubles partner—rushed to Jace's side. "Maybe he bailed," said Betsy. "Maybe he took off."

"But where would he go?"

Suddenly Rob Toretti, the student council president, grabbed Jace's arm. "Where is he?" Rob demanded. "He's gotta go up there."

"I don't know where he is," said Jace.

"This isn't funny," said Rob. "You gotta get him. He's the Prom King."

"I don't know where he is!" cried Jace. "He might have left. Let go of me."

"He can't *leave*," insisted Rob. "The Prom King can't *leave*."

Jace pulled away from Rob but more people had gathered around. Bethany hurried down from the stage and urged Jace to do something. "What do you want me to do?" said Jace, trying to get away.

"But you're his date!" said Bethany.

"So what?" said Jace.

"You have to do something. You have to make an announcement. People are waiting!"

People *were* waiting. Everywhere she looked, Jace was met by expectant, needy faces. "What kind of announcement?" she asked.

"Just that he's honored or whatever," said Bethany. "Or else we'll have to get a new Prom King."

A chant began somewhere in the room. *"Stoy-o! Stoy-o! Stoy-o!"*

"So get a new Prom King," hissed Jace. "It's not my fault!"

"You can't switch Prom Kings," said Rob Toretti, who wouldn't have minded being Prom King himself and was frankly a little offended that someone would throw away the honor.

"Just come onstage and say something," said Bethany.

"Just do it," said someone.

"I can't go up there," pleaded Jace. "What would I say?"

"You can accept it on his behalf. Like they do on TV."

Chloe had now fought her way into the crush of people pressed around Jace. When Rob Toretti wouldn't back away, Chloe kicked him.

"Ooww!" said Rob. "What are you doing!?"

Chloe and Betsy tried to pull Jace away from Rob and Bethany and the others. "Leave her alone!" barked Chloe. She kicked another boy, who howled and limped away.

Behind them a new chant had started. *"Tor-res, Tor-res, speech! speech! speech!"*

"If he's really gone," said Bethany, her face red, "you have to say something. You *have* to."

"Just say anything, so we can continue with the dance," said Rob Toretti, still grimacing from being kicked. "Do it for your school."

And so it was that Julia "Jace" Torres found herself onstage, at her prom, addressing her entire school.

"Uh . . ." she said into the microphone, as the brutal spotlight shone on her, making the top of her head hot and itchy.

Bethany stepped into the light and handed her a crown made of plastic jewels. *"On behalf of Paul . . ."* Bethany whispered to her.

"On behalf of Paul," repeated Jace, through the PA.

People laughed. Someone threw something. "The prom has two mommies!" yelled someone else.

"Show us the twins!"

"Uh, Paul had to go. . . ." mumbled Jace, swallowing dryly. "He doesn't really like crowds too much."

"Talk in the mike!" said someone.

"Speak up!"

Jace stood closer to the mike. She gathered her strength and spoke: "I just want to say that Paul . . . you know . . . he's a transfer and everything so he doesn't know that many of you, but he's really glad to be at our school and . . . he's glad that everyone supported him. . . ." She looked down at the plastic crown. She thought: *High school is so weird.* The tiniest bit of a smile crept onto her face. The crowd saw it and began laughing and cheering. Someone threw a red rose that landed at Jace's feet.

"So I guess that's it," said Jace. "Paul really loves being at Evergreen and thank you, from him."

"And *you* really love *Paul*!" shouted someone from the back. Everyone laughed. Everyone but Jace. She was mortified. She could feel the blood rush into her face. Bethany helped her off the stage. Behind them, a chant began: *"Paul and Jace! Paul and Jace! Paul and Jace!"*

Jace, in utter horror, fled across the dance floor to her table. She handed the crown to Chloe and untangled her purse and shawl from her chair.

Chloe handed the crown to Zach. Zach put it on. "I'll be Prom King," he said. "If you need one."

Abby punched him and caught the crown when it fell off his head. She handed it back to Jace.

Jace grabbed it. "I am *sooo* out of here," she declared. She snatched up the rest of her stuff.

"Where are you going?" Betsy asked her. "Do you want someone to come with you?"

Jace shook her head. Her face burned red with embarrassment.

"Are you sure?" said Chloe.

Jace was very sure.

Laura pushed forward. "Jace, are you okay?" she said. "Just tell us you're okay."

"I'm okay," said Jace.

"Don't be embarrassed," said Abby. "They're only kidding about you and Paul. They don't mean anything by it."

"You were great up there!" said Rebecca, not quite understanding what had happened.

Jace said nothing. The music began again. People streamed happily onto the dance floor. Jace took her things and stormed to the exit.

57

"You sure have a lot of drama at your school," Zach shouted to Chloe as they danced.

"So?"

"I'm not saying it's bad."

"What happens at your school?" asked Chloe. "Nothing?"

"Nah, stuff happens."

They danced. "Our school is usually boring," said Chloe, over the music. "You got lucky tonight."

The song ended, and a slow song began. Zach hesitated, as the couples around them embraced. "Do you wanna dance this one, too?"

"Do you?" said Chloe.

"Well yeah, if you do. I mean, if you don't want to dance with that Brian guy."

Chloe had danced the last slow-dance with Brian. "I told you," said Chloe. "He's just a friend."

"I know. But if you'd rather . . ."

"Just come here," said Chloe, lifting her arms.

Zach carefully placed his hands on her waist. Chloe moved closer. She hung her wrists loosely around his neck and let the side of her head rest on Zach's shoulder.

For a few moments, the two cautiously shuffled in a slow circle.

"Are you having fun?" Chloe finally asked, a soft R&B song thumping behind them.

"Yeah," said Zach.

"Are you glad you came?"

"Yeah."

Chloe shifted her grip on him slightly. He shifted his grip on her. They settled into each other a little more. New parts of their bodies touched.

"How about you?" whispered Zach, into the top of her head. "Are you having an okay time?"

"Yeah. . . ." said Chloe. Her hips moved with the music. Zach moved with her.

"You smell good," said Zach, in a low voice. He closed his eyes and breathed in the side of her head.

"Were you afraid to come?" asked Chloe, abruptly lifting her head to look at him. "Did you think I was weird on the phone?"

"No."

"What did Abby tell you about me?"

"Nothing. That you were cute," said Zach.

Chloe rested her head on his chest again. "Do you think I am?"

"Yeah, I guess so."

"You guess so?"

Zach stroked her hair once to reassure her. "You're pretty cute," said Zach. "And you're fun, at least."

"I know," said Chloe, settling back into his shoulder. "You are, too, kinda. You sure sweat a lot."

"So you're glad I came?"

"Yes," said Chloe.

"I know we just met," said Zach. "But I feel like I could say stuff to you. Like you wouldn't freak out."

"Me, too."

"Actually, there's something I want to ask you," he said.

"What?"

"I dunno. Maybe I shouldn't."

"What is it?" asked Chloe.

"Maybe I should just do it instead."

Zach moved his face in front of Chloe's face. He studied the contours of her face and then gently kissed her cheek. At first she did nothing. She kept her head still. She watched him.

But when he moved lower with his mouth, she lifted her lips to his. She kissed him. On the lips. She did it once, slowly, softly.

It lasted a second or two. Then they settled back into their original positions. Now there was no talking, no teasing. There was just thinking, and breathing, and pressing against the other person.

58

Naturally, after Paul won Prom King, Mike disappeared again. He had apparently gone back upstairs. Laura had seen Daniel and Christine and several other seniors on the dance floor; the "private" party must have thinned out. Laura decided this might be a good time to make an appearance.

She wound her way out of the ballroom and into the main hallway. She found the stairwell, which had a small sign beside it that actually said, "VIP Room." Mike and Daniel must have loved that. She opened the door and found herself in a lush, dark, carpeted stairwell. She lifted her dress and began to climb the stairs. She was halfway up when Sarah Vandeway and some of her friends came rushing down. Laura smiled at Sarah and tried to congratulate her. But Sarah was preoccupied with dramas of her own and ignored her. So did her friends. *Thanks a lot,* thought Laura. *So glad I voted for you.*

When she reached the top of the stairs, Laura was pleasantly surprised to find herself in an elegant lounge. It was supposed to be a bar, but the liquor part was locked up. Still, it had that dark, low-ceiling look of a nightclub you might see in a movie or TV show. It really was a VIP area.

There were parents, of course. They were standing in a group around the top of the stairs. Except for them, and about a dozen seniors standing at a window overlooking the dance floor, it appeared pretty empty. She probably should have come up earlier. She probably missed something.

She walked toward the center of the room. In the dim light she saw some more people sitting on a couch. There was a couple in a darkened booth, cuddling and sneaking kisses. Another group of four senior boys stood next to a colorful aquarium. It all seemed a little pretentious and unnecessary to Laura, but that's how the seniors had been all year. Trying too hard to be sophisticated and cool. "Las Vegas" was the theme of the yearbook that year.

Laura searched for Mike. As she moved through the long room she saw that there were little alcoves, with tables or love seats here and there, some lit by candles, some not lit at all. It was also colder up here: the air-conditioning gave her goose bumps, made her appreciate the feel of her sheer dress on her bare skin. When she unexpectedly caught sight of herself in a darkened mirror, she was shocked at how sexy and grown-up she looked. Maybe VIP rooms weren't so bad after all.

But where was Mike? When Laura reached one end of the lounge area, she turned and went the other way. Three breathless girls had just appeared at the top of the stairwell; she moved around them and walked toward the other end of the lounge area.

There was no one at that end. It was dark and completely deserted. She turned to leave, but thought she heard a male voice. It came from one of the alcoves, along the far wall. Laura crept forward, just enough to see. There was someone there, at the table. It was . . . *Mike*. The candle was out, but she could see the stark whiteness of his tux shirt, and the unfastened tie that hung from his neck. Who was he talking to? And why was he sitting in that odd position?

Laura stepped forward, then stopped. There was a hand around his neck. A female hand. There was someone sitting beside him.

"No . . ." giggled a girl's voice. "Not here."

"Why not?" murmured Mike. "No one can see. . . ."

There was a pause while something physical happened that Laura couldn't see.

Then Marianne's hard, husky voice: "You're *bad*," she breathed.

"You're the bad one," whispered Mike.

The words hit Laura like a blow to the stomach. She lurched silently backward, a trembling hand over her nose and mouth. She backed into a table, faltered, almost fell.

Behind her, the seniors by the aquarium burst out laughing.

59

Once she'd escaped the main ballroom, Jace wasn't sure where to go. She wasn't sure she wanted to see Paul. She had a vague idea of walking all the way home. Or calling her brothers.

But outside, her feet steered her back to the parking garage. That's where Paul would be, hiding in his car. She held her dress up and climbed the cement stairs, surprising a couple making out in the stairwell. On the fourth floor, she marched across the concrete to Paul's Suburban. She couldn't see anyone through the tinted windows. Maybe Paul was on the floor. She stepped closer and looked in. No Paul. She tried the doors. They were locked. Far across the parking garage some other prom people stood around a car. Paul wasn't among them.

But he was here, somewhere—Jace could feel it. Remembering the trick of checking under the stalls in the girls' bathroom, she lifted her dress farther and knelt down on the rough cement between the cars. She bent her head to the ground and looked under the cars. Sure enough, several cars to her left, she saw a boy's shoe and a pant leg. As quietly as she could, she circled around the

Suburban and walked in that direction. Four cars later she found Paul. He was between cars, sitting on the ground, his back to the cement wall. His knees were up, his head down, and he was flicking little rocks with his fingers.

"Paul?" said Jace.

He looked up. "Oh, hey."

"What are you doing?"

He shrugged. "Nothing. I needed some air."

Jace's anger returned to her. "I thought you were going to tell me if you wanted to leave," she said.

"Oh," said Paul. "I guess I forgot."

"You *forgot*? Well, thanks for thinking of me."

"Someone told me I might get voted Prom King," said Paul. "Can you believe that? So I bailed."

Jace glared at him. "Well, they were right. You were voted Prom King. And here's your crown." She threw it at him.

It bounced on the cement in front of him. One of the plastic jewels fell off. Paul stared at it for a moment. He picked it up. "Are you serious? I won this?"

"Yes."

He studied it for a moment. "Wow," he said.

"Yeah, *wow*," said Jace.

Paul looked at her. "Why are you so pissed off?"

"Do you have any idea what happened to me back there?"

"No," he said. "What happened?"

"I just got totally . . ." Suddenly, she looked like she might cry.

Paul saw this and scrambled to his feet. "What? What happened?"

"Nothing," said Jace, turning away. "Just . . . everyone . . ."

"Oh my God," said Paul, with sudden concern. "Was it something I did? Was it my fault?"

"It wasn't your fault," sniffed Jace. "It was . . . well . . . it was kind of your fault."

"I'm so sorry. What happened? Tell me."

Jace shook her head. "People said things."

"What did they say? Who said it?"

"They teased me. They said I was . . . that you and I . . . that we should be together."

"Who said it?" said Paul.

"A lot of people."

"Like who? Like a big group?"

"A *very* big group."

"How big?" said Paul. "Like a whole table?"

"No. Like, the whole school."

Paul was not understanding this. "You mean like Chloe and those guys?"

"No, I mean the *whole school*!" said Jace with emphasis. "I had to go onstage and accept your, your stupid kingship or whatever. And then they started yelling things. And then they started chanting, 'Paul and Jace! Paul and Jace!' Like a basketball game."

Paul almost laughed. He couldn't help himself. Then he straightened his face. "Oh, I'm sorry, that must have been terrible."

Jace sort of laughed, too. But then she straightened her face also. "It was *totally embarrassing*," she said. "And to have everyone in the whole school chanting that, knowing that, *agreeing* with that, and where are you? Hiding in the parking lot!"

Paul became genuinely serious when he heard that. He let go of Jace. He stepped back from her.

"And now," said Jace. "Now, you're going to freak out and claim you can only like me as a friend or you're not ready, or you don't want to hurt me, or some other excuse. And I'll go home and you'll go home and nothing will ever happen because you're too afraid—"

"Jace," said Paul. "You gotta believe me. It was very serious what happened to me. I don't think you understand."

"Understand what? That you have problems? That some really bad things have happened to you?" She turned and confronted him. "Well guess what, my mother died when I was twelve. And I've had to live my whole life with four men. And besides that, I'm Mexican. People look down on me everywhere I go, every day of my life. And guess what, I can still care about people!"

"I'm not saying I can't care about people," said Paul.

"Then what are you saying?"

"I'm just saying, I wouldn't make a very good . . . boyfriend. . . ."

"I'm not asking you to be my boyfriend. I'm just asking you to be open. And let things evolve without judging, or deciding ahead of time how you're going to feel."

"But what if something went wrong? What if I had to go back to the hospital? My problems are so different."

"Yeah," said Jace. "I'm sure they are different. But you know what? *I'll take my chances.* Just like you'll have to take your chances with my problems. That's what you do, Paul. That's what everyone has to do."

Paul stared down at his crown, which he still held in his hands. Jace took it from him. It was broken, bent, and several of the plastic jewels were missing. "That's the thing about you, Paul," said Jace, in a softer voice. "You really are a king. But you gotta be brave. And you can't be afraid to take what is yours."

60

By 10:40, Zach and Chloe had had enough prom. They decided to go exploring. They slipped through a door beside the stage they saw the DJ using. It led to a maze of tunnels and passageways that eventually took them to an enormous empty kitchen. Here they swatted and spanked each other with cooking utensils and ate some stale cupcakes they found that said "Class of '97!" Next they discovered a huge laundry room where Chloe jumped in a pile of what turned out to be dirty towels.

Eventually they let themselves out through an emergency exit and found themselves in an alley behind the hotel. Unsure of what to do next, they headed up the hill toward the Portland State campus, where the big fountain was. The cherry blossoms along the sidewalk moved gently in the breeze. Cars passed on the street. They walked several feet apart, without speaking, each of them needing space, needing a period of adjustment, a moment to consider what had happened to them so far and what might happen still.

When they reached the campus lawn, Chloe took off her shoes. They strolled through the grass toward the big fountain. Other prom-goers had come here, too. It was a natural place to gather. A group of flushed prom girls stood in a row taking pictures.

Zach and Chloe circled the fountain. "So what kind of poems did you write about me?" he asked.

"None of your business," answered Chloe.

"You really wrote thirty-seven poems?"

"Thirty-one."

"That's a lot of poems."

"You were very flexible then. There were a lot of directions I could go with you."

Zach smiled. "So what were they about?'

"I told you, it's none of your business,' said Chloe. "It's not polite to ask someone what they wrote about you."

Zach looked down at her. "Yeah, well it's not polite to

tell someone you wrote poems about them and refuse to tell what they're about."

"You don't know very much about the creative process do you?" said Chloe, looking around at the dark trees.

"And besides, since when are you the expert on what's polite?" asked Zach.

"I am perfectly polite when I want to be," said Chloe.

"Yeah, when you *want* to be."

"What is that supposed to mean?"

"Nothing," said Zach. "It's just obvious you do whatever the hell you want, whenever you want to."

Chloe stopped walking. She turned to him. "That's not a very nice thing to say about a person."

"But it's true. Isn't it?"

"How do you know if it's true or not? You don't know me. Take it back."

"I'm just saying, you're a very honest person," said Zach.

"Take it back."

"Why? I'm right," said Zach, with quiet firmness.

Chloe stepped forward and kicked him in the shin.

"Ooww," said Zach, jumping back. He hobbled for a moment. "What was that for?"

Chloe stared at him.

"You just *kicked* me," said Zach.

"So? It wasn't very hard," said Chloe.

"It wasn't very *hard*?" said Zach. "What difference does that make?"

Chloe said nothing.

"Listen," said Zach, rubbing his leg. "Let's get one thing straight. No *kicking*. Okay? Are we clear on that?"

Chloe watched him with her large green eyes.

"I'm serious," said Zach. "There will be no kicking in this relationship. All right?"

Chloe thought about the word *relationship*. She wondered what it meant, how far it reached, what it did to a person to be *in a relationship*. Then she stepped forward and kicked him again.

"Owww!" said Zach, hopping on his other leg. "You just kicked me again! Are you crazy?"

Chloe studied Zach as if he were a specimen under glass.

"If you do that again," said Zach, angrily pointing a finger at her, "I swear to God, I'll . . ."

"What?" said Chloe.

"I'll . . . I'll throw you in that fountain!"

"You will?"

"Yes, I will."

Chloe looked into the fountain. Fresh water poured from its top as spotlights illuminated the mist. Chloe stepped forward and kicked him a third time.

"That's it!" said Zach.

"Aaaaaahhhhhhhhh!!!!!!!!" screamed Chloe as she took off running around the fountain. Zach limped after her. Chloe was faster than she looked. It took almost two complete laps of the fountain before Zach even got close to her. By then she was laughing hysterically. When she made a dash for the woods, he caught her, tackled her, and they both tumbled onto the soft grass. At first, they were breathing so hard they lay unmoving on the ground. Chloe had lost her shoes. Zach had a huge green stain on one knee of his tuxedo. When she'd caught her breath, Chloe sprang to her feet and ran for the trees. Zach jumped up and tackled her again. They struggled on the ground, in the dirt, in the pine needles. Chloe squirmed and struggled, but finally Zach caught both her wrists and pinned her to the ground.

Chloe gazed up into his eyes. Zach, his chest heaving, stared at her lips. He lowered himself until his face was inches from hers. He breathed on her, let his eyes close, and finally kissed her delicate lips. She kissed him back, kissed him in a different way, as if their fates were joined now, as if some new door had been opened, some new difficult adventure had been laid out before them.

Then Zach picked her up, carried her to the fountain, and threw her in.

61

Pushing out through the VIP room door, Laura found herself in the crowded main hall outside the ballroom. It was ten minutes after eleven, the dance was over, and a mass of chattering prom-goers was migrating toward the exits.

Laura stood surrounded by sweaty faces, glowing smiles. People talked, shouted, gathered themselves into groups. Laura had so internalized the schedule that her first thought was after-parties. She knew of some, though she had planned to do whatever Mike wanted. That was the compromise she had made in her head: If he would put up with her friends early in the night, she'd do what he wanted later.

None of that mattered now. There were no schedules, no deals, no compromises. There was nothing. Laura was floating now. It was a new world.

She walked forward into the crowd. Someone said hi to her. Someone else asked her a question. She didn't answer. She shuffled forward, following people down the main hallway. At the end of it, she broke away from those going to the parking garage and strode toward the front, through the main lobby, passing a family on vacation, a group of Japanese businessmen, a red-coated hotel porter.

Now she was on the street. Alone. She walked aimlessly, staring blankly at taxis, pedestrians, cars waiting at the curb. She had no idea what she was doing or where she was going. Still, people smiled at her—tourists, couples, people out for an evening stroll. Everyone loved a girl in a prom dress, even one with tears in her eyes.

A limousine stopped in front of her. Laura turned to avoid the people getting out. She walked with her head down. She would talk to Mike. They would discuss what happened. They would break up. Of course they would.

He had left her no choice. They would meet somewhere and discuss it. What happened. Why. Or would they? What if they didn't? School was basically over. He was a senior. *What if she never talked to him again?*

That thought broke her. A wave of pain shot through her chest. She doubled over and started to cry. She struggled to control herself. She straightened up again, walked faster, but the tears came in a rush, and they streamed down her cheeks. She needed to get off the street. Where were Jace and Chloe? Where was she? Laura looked down at her 349-dollar prom dress and saw that the bottom was already filthy. She had not intended to wander the city streets in it. She had intended to do what? Go with Mike. Be with Mike. Do what Mike said. Have sex with Mike when Mike told her to. Her face broke apart, and she sobbed loudly. But she was in public. On the street. People could see her. She covered her mouth with her hand and steadied herself against a building. Far ahead of her she saw people in prom clothes. They were heading uphill, toward Portland State, to the fountain. If she could get there, if she could find her friends . . .

62

Chloe was not drunk. But you wouldn't know that by looking at her.

She stood in the middle of a dark lawn, shoeless and

soaking wet. Her plastic hair barrette was gone, her purse was gone, her hair hung off her like a sea-hag. She had once again escaped from Zach and run away, barefoot, with his white tuxedo coat over her shoulders. In her reckless flight, she had traveled the length of the Portland State campus and now stood unsteadily, completely winded, and in search of a place to sit down.

Across the grass from her was an unlit tennis court. There she saw something she didn't quite understand. She saw a girl in a prom dress playing . . . *basketball*? She looked again and saw it was true; a basketball hoop hung at the end of the tennis court and two people were playing on it, a girl in a light colored gown and a boy in a tux. She strained to see them in the dark. Were the two people *kissing*?

Chloe watched them. The girl broke away from the boy and dribbled the ball. She threw it to the boy and he shot it toward the basket. Then they started kissing again. What a weird thing to do after a prom. Then the girl moved a certain way Chloe recognized. Could it be . . . *Jace*?

Paul couldn't believe his eyes when Chloe walked onto the court. At first he thought she had lost her dress. But, in fact, it was still there; it was just wet and stuck to her, so that she looked like one of those disaster victims on CNN.

"Chloe?" said Jace, who was about to shoot a basket,

but turned to look at whatever Paul was staring at.

Chloe, barefoot and huddled in Zach's coat, stared back. "What are you guys doing?"

"Nothing. Shooting baskets," said Jace.

"What are *you* doing?" said Paul, walking quickly across the court to her. "What happened to you?"

"Nothing," said Chloe. "Zach threw me in the fountain."

"Oh my God," said Jace, now hurrying, too. "You're soaking wet! And you're practically naked!"

"No, I'm not," said Chloe, calmly. "I have my dress on."

"I'll get a blanket from the car," said Paul, running to his Suburban, which was parked beside the court.

"Chloe," said Jace, putting her arms around her, "you're freezing. You're shivering!"

Chloe looked down at herself. She *had* gotten cold since she stopped running. She felt her chin and lower lip tremble.

"Where's Zach?" said Jace.

"He was trying to catch me. I got away."

"Why are you running away from him?"

"I don't know. It was fun. He was chasing me."

Paul's car door made a buzz when it opened. Jace and Chloe both watched him for a moment. Then Chloe touched Jace's arm. "I think I love Zach," she said quietly.

"You do?" said Jace. "But you just met him."

"I know. That's what's so scary about it."

"How do you know?" asked Jace.

"I just . . . I just want to run away from him forever and I want him to always be trying to catch me."

"Chloe, that's weird."

"He's all inside me now. I can feel it."

Jace looked her up and down. "People in love are supposed to look good, not be naked and wet and—where are you shoes?"

Chloe looked down. "I lost them."

"Your big toe is bleeding!"

"I was running through the woods."

"And your hair, and your dress, and your. . . . Oh, Chloe," said Jace, hugging her in her arms. "Oh, *Chloe*."

63

With the heat on and Chloe wrapped in a blanket, Paul steered the Suburban toward the lower campus where the fountain was, where they would hopefully find Zach. At the fountain a large crowd of prom people had gathered. Zach was not among them.

Paul left the Suburban running and the heat on. He and Jace walked across the grass toward the fountain. Paul circled around one way, Jace went the other. "Zach!" Paul called into the trees.

As they searched, Jace watched Paul across the grass. He was so handsome. And loyal. And the first to try to help someone. She was not going to let Paul go. She could feel it now, stronger than she ever had. *Paul and Jace!* they had chanted. And they were right.

Then she walked into Laura. She practically crashed into her. "Oh!" said Jace with surprise. "Laura! What are you doing here?"

"I was just walking," said Laura. "I was looking for you guys."

Jace couldn't see her face in the dark. "Where's Mike? Aren't you guys going to the after-parties?"

"I don't think so. . . ." said Laura. She took a breath. "He's back at the hotel."

"Is he meeting you here?"

"No," said Laura, her voice filling with emotion. "I don't think I'll be . . . hanging out with Mike anymore."

"What?" said Jace. "Oh no, what happened?"

Laura shook her head.

"Did something . . . did you guys break up?"

"I think we did."

"Oh, Laura," said Jace. She took her friend by the hand. "Oh my God. I'm *so sorry*."

At that moment, Jace heard a sudden rush of footsteps on the cement path behind her. "There you are!" boomed a voice. Jace turned and saw Zach running up the hill toward the Suburban. Chloe stood in the grass beside it, wrapped in her blanket. "Where did you go!?" said Zach.

Jace and Laura both watched Zach take Chloe in his

arms. "Stop running away!" he said. "Jesus, you scared me to death!"

"At least one good thing came out of this night," said Laura, quietly.

Jace squeezed her hand. "Actually, two good things."

"You and Paul?"

Jace nodded.

"I'm so glad," said Laura.

"And all of this was your idea. You did this for us."

Laura managed a weak smile for her friend.

64

In the Suburban, the five friends headed home. Paul and Jace sat in the front seat. Zach and soggy Chloe were in the back. Laura sat beside them by the window.

Though Chloe was now dry enough to tease Zach, she did not. She had been told about Laura and Mike and so kept quiet. Everyone in the car maintained a stony silence, out of respect for Laura's tragic situation. Laura for her part was actually feeling a little better. She had cried in the street, cried at the fountain, cried in the car, and now felt an unexpected relief, though she continued to dab at her eyes with a Dairy Queen napkin Zach had found in his coat pocket.

It was only twelve thirty, but Paul—not knowing what

else to do—found himself driving in the direction of Chloe's house. He would take everyone home. That seemed to be what people wanted. And no one had suggested anything else.

As they drove, Zach's cell phone rang. He wasn't sure if he should answer it and break the mournful silence, but Chloe poked him and he did. "Hello?" he said. "Hey, Abby. . . . Nothing. . . . We're heading home I guess. . . . Yeah? . . . Huh. . . . Okay. . . . I don't think so. . . . Maybe. . . . All right."

He hung up.

"What did she want?" said Chloe in a somber voice.

"She just wanted to check in."

"What's she doing?" said Jace.

"They're all going to Denny's."

"To Denny's?" said Jace, glancing at Laura. "That's not much of a finish to prom night."

"I guess a bunch of them are going," said Zach. He said to Chloe, "Your friend Rebecca is with them. And Brian."

"Really?" said Chloe. But then for Laura's sake she lowered her voice again. "Still, it's only Denny's," she said. "We might as well go home."

Laura cleared her throat. "If you guys want to go to Denny's you should," she said. "I can go home."

"No way," said Jace. "We're not leaving you."

"Who wants to go to Denny's? Yuck!" said Chloe, though it was obvious to everyone she wanted to go.

"We've had enough excitement," said Paul.

"Actually," said Laura, still dabbing at her eyes, "I wouldn't mind getting something to eat myself. I haven't eaten in two days."

"But you don't want to go to Denny's," said Jace. "Not in that beautiful dress."

"It doesn't matter. And I don't want to keep you guys," said Laura.

"Are you sure?" said Jace.

"Yeah," said Chloe. "Are you sure?"

"Yes," said Laura. "I am sure. I want to go."

Paul changed lanes and pulled into a parking lot so he could turn around.

"Abby said some guy named Ryan was there," added Zach. "From a pet store? She said you guys know him."

"Ryan?" said Chloe.

"From the mall?" said Jace.

Laura said nothing. She stared out the window and dabbed her eyes with her napkin.

65

At Denny's, after everyone had ordered, Chloe was sent to the bathroom to wash off her bleeding toe.

Chloe was no expert on first aid. But she did her best. She locked the door of the restroom and hopped awkwardly on one bare foot, managing to get her foot into the sink. She turned on the water and rinsed the mud and grass off it. She was lucky she had even gotten into Denny's without shoes. She had hidden behind Zach when they entered.

She had most of her foot clean when someone knocked on the door. "How's it going in there?" asked Jace.

"Not that good," said Chloe, hopping to the door. She let Jace in and quickly hopped back to the sink again.

"Where's the cut?" said Jace, relocking the door.

"On my big toe," said Chloe.

"Does it hurt?"

"Not really," said Chloe. She swung her foot back onto the edge of the sink.

Jace helped, letting Chloe grip her shoulder for stability, while she dabbed at the cut with a paper towel.

"How's it going out there with Ryan and Laura?" whispered Chloe. Part of the reason Chloe had agreed to wash her foot was to rearrange the booth seating so Laura and Ryan would sit together.

"They're talking," said Jace. "He sure was glad to see her."

Chloe almost slipped on the wet floor. Jace held her up.

"These aren't exactly sanitary conditions," said Jace, grabbing more paper towels.

There was another knock on the door.

"Don't come in," said Chloe. "We're just washing off my toe."

"What are you washing it with?" asked Laura, through the door.

"Water," said Chloe, lowering her foot. "We're fine. Go back to the table."

"You need to use soap. And you need to wash it thoroughly. Let me in."

Jace let her in. Laura immediately went to work on Chloe's big toe. She made Chloe put it in the sink and thoroughly cleaned it, this time using soap and paper towels from the dispenser. Jace and Chloe watched.

Then Jace spoke up. "How's Ryan?" she asked.

"Okay," said Laura, dutifully scrubbing the toe. It obviously calmed Laura to help her friend.

"He sure likes you," added Chloe, cautiously.

"Not that you would like him," Jace added quickly. "I mean you'll need time to get over Mike."

"Yeah," agreed Chloe. "You'll need lots of time."

"He asked me to his prom," said Laura, without looking up.

"He *did*?" said Jace. "Like, right now he did?"

"Two minutes ago," said Laura.

Chloe and Jace stared at each other with wide eyes.

"Are you going to go?" asked Jace.

"I don't think so," said Laura. "It's next week."

"Wait, can you go to two proms?" asked Chloe.

"He said it wouldn't have to be a big deal," said Laura. "We would just go as friends or whatever."

"You could *totally* go as friends," said Jace. "That would be great. It would help get your mind off Mike."

"Yeah," said Chloe. "Maybe you should do it."

"Still," said Laura. "I wouldn't have anything to wear. This dress is ruined."

"What about mine?" said Jace. "You could have mine."

"Or you could go to the vintage place," said Chloe. "Their stuff is cheap."

"I don't know," said Laura. "Normally I wouldn't even consider it. How could I? But then I think, who's stopping me? Why not? And he needs a date."

"Exactly!" said Jace. "You're just helping a friend. And why not?"

"I still don't see how you can go to two proms," said Chloe.

"I don't know," said Laura. "It might be too much. I'll have to think about it." She delicately set down Chloe's foot.

For the first time Laura looked around at the dirty restroom. "God, look at us," said Laura. "In the Denny's bathroom on prom night. This isn't exactly where I thought we'd end up."

"I don't mind it," said Chloe. "I like Denny's."

"At least we're together," said Jace.

Laura smiled. Jace took her hand. Then the three girls moved together for a group hug. It seemed like a good time for one. Especially since Chloe was still hopping on one foot and was about to fall over.

66

"I told you Mike Gardner was a rapist!" said Shawnie, as she lay on the floor of the world history section.

"He didn't *rape* Marianne," said Chloe, lying beside her. "He *hooked up* with her. He was probably hooking up with her all along."

"I heard he and Daniel Weiss got in a huge fight at an after-party," said Rebecca.

"Good," said Shawnie. "I hope all those assholes kill each other."

"I heard Daniel was crying and all freaking out and stuff," said Rebecca, who had followed the post-prom gossip closely. She was entitled to follow it. She had been there.

"The thing I don't understand," said Chloe, "is how can Laura go to two proms? Isn't that like getting married twice?"

"God, Chloe," said Shawnie. "Do you know anything about anything?"

"I'm serious," said Chloe. "If you can go to a million proms with a million different people, why is it so important? How can it be a 'once in a lifetime' event? And why do people spend so much money on it?"

"Because," said Shawnie, "people are idiots."

"I didn't spend any money on it, and I had fun," said Rebecca. "I didn't even buy a ticket."

"Yeah, well you went with a gay guy," said Shawnie.

"That doesn't make it any less valid," said Rebecca, who had gained a bit of confidence by going to the prom.

Shawnie scribbled irritably in her notebook. Chloe drew a picture of Zach next to a list of possible names for their children, which included Paisley, Edith, and Sylvia.

Suddenly, a new presence entered the world history aisle.

"Whoaa! You're actually here!" said a large, spongy-haired male, as he bounded over the sprawled bodies of Shawnie and Chloe. "So you really do hang out here with your geek friends!"

The three girls stared at the large intruder.

"How did you find us?" said Chloe, rolling onto her side.

"You said the world history section of the Barnes & Noble. How could I *not* find you?"

Shawnie glared at him. "For your information, who-ever you are, we are not *geeks.*"

"Zach Skinner, pleased to meet you!" said huge, irre-pressible Zach. He knelt down to the level of the girls. "And I don't mean 'geeks' in a bad way. I mean 'geeks' in a smart, ironic way."

"Yeah, right," Shawnie grumbled.

Chloe started to speak but became tongue-tied.

Zach turned to her. "Anyway, the reason I came. I don't know what your plans for the day are. But I got my dad's truck. And it's gonna get hot later. I was thinking we could go to the river. It's usually pretty cool down there on Saturdays."

The girls weren't sure who he meant.

"Who?" said Chloe. "All of us?"

"Of course. If you all want to go."

"I don't like water," said Shawnie.

"Yeah?" said Zach. "You can lay out on the rocks then. It's fun. Lots of people go. Whaddaya think?"

It sounded good to Chloe. Rebecca couldn't think of a reason to say no. Shawnie was actually a little bored herself, though she would never admit it.

"It's settled then," said Zach, rising to his full height. He held out a hand to Chloe, who took it and was effortlessly lifted to her feet. He did the same for Rebecca. He held out a hand to Shawnie. She did not take it. She glared up at him. "No thank you," she said. "I don't need help *standing up*."

"Oh, I do think you need help," said Chloe, a slightly mischievous edge in her voice.

"Yeah," said Rebecca. "I think Zach might need to help you get up."

"I said no thanks," muttered Shawnie, still lying on the floor. "I don't even want to go."

"Zach, would you do us a huge favor and put Shawnie in your truck?" said Chloe.

"Sure," said Zach, and in one smooth motion he picked Shawnie up and flung her over his shoulder.

Naturally, there was some screaming, a little swearing, a bit of pounding on Zach's back. But nobody at Barnes & Noble seemed particularly concerned about it. In fact, the employees were glad to see the three girls going somewhere else for a change. It was summertime; young girls shouldn't be hanging around a bookstore all day. Besides, it would be nice to have some access to the world history section for a change. Who knew? Maybe an actual customer might venture there.